HOSTILE ATTRACTIONS

RALEIGH DAVIS

It's raining so hard I'm not sure if I'm still on the sidewalk or if I've somehow ended up in the Third Street canal.

When people think of San Francisco, they usually imagine fog and cold and hills, and they wouldn't be wrong. Rain doesn't usually figure, at least not a hard rain. But sometimes it pours here like cats and dogs, backing up the storm drains until you have no choice but to wade through knee-high rivers.

Tonight it's coming down so fast and thick I can't even see the streetlights, and I'm soaked to the skin, shivering under my suit. Water pools in my shoes, which squelch with every step. I'm miserable, from the dripping-wet roots of my hair to the tips of my freezing toes.

Weather-wise, this is the worst possible night for me to run. I could drown out here. But in some ways, it's the best night for me to run. My boss doesn't like the rain, so he won't venture out of his estate. Won't wander into the office and wonder why I'm suddenly gone, won't notice someone's been downloading files from his private computer.

I shouldn't be cursing the rain since it's a blessing.

Cars crawl down Channel Street, trying to drive between the sheets of water and gusts of wind. Their windshield wipers are going full speed, pushing off the rain as fast as it lands. I'm the only person foolish enough to be walking here.

I'm surrounded by water. Above me, below me, and just to my right, an entire canal, which surprises people some-times—a canal in San Francisco. Across the Bay, of course, there's the great port of Oakland with cranes and shipping containers and the massive tankers endlessly churning through it.

San Francisco used to be a massive port city too, although now the only boats here are ferries and yachts—toys for commuters, tourists, and rich people. The Third Street canal is left over from those days, and it holds the kind of boats you'd never expect to find in San Francisco—houseboats.

My hand grips the railing tightly, the only thing preventing me from being blown off the sidewalk by the wind and swept right into the canal. I feel my way forward, gritting my eyes against the rain lashing my face. I've already passed El Dorado Street, so the gate to the dock should be coming up any moment now. I can't see it, not with the rain swallowing the light from the streetlamps and the headlights, so I pray I'll be able to recognize it by touch. I also pray that the dock gate is somehow, against all odds, unlocked. Nothing in San Francisco is ever unlocked though.

If the gate *is* locked, I pray that I can pick it. I used to be really good at that, but I'm out of practice. And sitting out in the rain jimmying a lock would draw too much attention.

I shrink farther into myself, shivering. I can't attract any attention. Not when every camera in the city could be searching for me. I know where they all are—I helped install them—so I've done my best to avoid them, but I was also very good at my job, and I made sure nearly every inch of the city was blanketed.

The rain will help. I tremble again, my entire body clenching. My muscles ache from the cold and the shivering, and I still haven't found the gate.

Not that there's likely to be anything close to warmth waiting for me when I arrive. But I have no choice.

The metal of the railing is like ice, hard and slick. My fingers lost feeling somewhere back near the Third Street Bridge, but I keep pulling myself forward.

My hands encounter something different from the endless railing, a bar of metal that rises up and up. I let my fingers slide over the bar and find something hard and raised and round. A dead bolt.

I found the gate. I don't allow myself even a breath of relief. There's no time.

With my left hand hanging on to the dead bolt, I use my right to check beneath my shirt, making sure the hard drive is still safe. I *know* it's still there because it's massive and heavy and tucked awkwardly into the band of my bra, but I spent the past five years collecting what's on that drive. I'm risking everything to steal it. If it's lost...

But it's not. The hard plastic rectangle about the size of a book, carrying eight terabytes of information all packed into a single plastic case, is still stuffed beneath my clothes. Eight terabytes that are going to bring down one of the most evil corporations in the world.

I feel my way down the dead bolt to the handle of the gate, trying to figure out how I'm going to pick this lock. My hair is plastered over my face, glued to my skin by the wind. There's no way I'll get a good view.

I push my finger against the keyhole. It feels like—

The gate swings inward, rusty hinges screaming over the wind. Looks like I won't have to pick anything at all.

I reach for the railing past the gate, the one attached to the ramp leading down to the dock, and slowly, with tiny mincing steps, make my way down. I can hear the water of the canal under my feet, sloshing angrily. Like it's mad it can't get at me.

I swallow hard and try to go faster. I've never really liked water or boats, so it makes perfect sense that this is where Elliot Martell would be. Elliot absolutely hates me.

But he hates my boss more. That is exactly the thing I'm counting on to keep me safe here.

The wind rushes between the buildings lining the canal and gusts along the surface of the water, catching the ramp and making it vibrate beneath my feet. I hold tight to the railing and swallow my scream.

It seems to take hours, but finally the ramp levels out and I'm actually on the pier. Problem is, the railing ends where the pier begins, and I have nothing more to cling to. I can only wrap my arms tight around myself, tuck my chin into my chest, and push forward through the wind. I can see vague shadows in the water, which I'm guessing are the houseboats. They don't seem to be moving at all, which I find odd. Shouldn't boats be bobbing with the water?

My breath starts to go sharp, jerky. In the dark, all the boats look the same. Black and hulking, with none of the interior lights on.

I found Elliot's address in the company database, complete with satellite photos. But here in the dark, I have no way to figure out which one is his short of shouting his name.

If he knows I'm coming, he'll lock the door against me. He might even push me into the canal himself.

For the first time since I started this entire... *thing*, I doubt my plan. After five years of pretending to be someone else, of saying and doing things that were completely against everything I'd believed in before, now... now I falter. I've got the hard drive under my shirt, but my legs aren't moving any longer. My knees want to crumple, but I lock them tight. I can't give up. Not now.

I notice a light then, at the very end of the dock, or at least what I assume is the end of the dock. In this weather, it's hard to tell where the dock ends and the water begins. But it's the only light I can see, so I head toward it.

The wind and rain seem to grow in strength as I move toward the light—Mother Nature herself is trying to flatten me. If I were superstitious, I'd say it's a sign I'm making a huge mistake. But I'm not superstitious.

Wait, scratch that. I did used to be superstitious. *Minerva* is not superstitious. I am…

Instinctively I squash that thought. Being anything other than Minerva is too dangerous. *Was* too dangerous.

Hell, I don't know anymore.

I focus on the light, which reveals itself to be a window in a door as it grows, a single square of cheery yellow in the bleak, black rain. I don't know if it's Elliot's boat, but I don't have a choice. The longer I stay out here, the more likely it is the hard drive will get ruined. Or that Fuchs will track me down.

I'm pretty sure that when he finds out what I've done, he'll want me dead. And not in an "Oh, I wish I could kill her but obviously I can't" kind of way. No, my life will be in very real danger. And with the people he knows in the CIA and the NSA—the people he *controls* there—it will be very easy for him to make me disappear.

No one would ever notice, because Minerva Dyne has nothing in her life except her job.

The light looks so welcoming when I reach it, the only spot of warmth in the dark wet. But I'll have to step off the dock and over the water in order to get on the boat and to that light. It's just one step, but I can't make myself do it.

Suddenly my old fear of boats and open water comes crashing back, filling my chest, my lungs, my throat. I'm going to drown on dry land. I know it.

I close my eyes tight. *Minerva is not afraid of boats. Minerva is not afraid of anything.* I can't stop shaking. I can't do this. I can't step over that water, because it's dark and cold and I'll miss the boat and sink down to the bottom.

No one will ever find me. No one will ever look.

The door opens, light spilling out and illuminating the ship's deck. A man's body is outlined in the doorway. His broad shoulders and long legs take up most of the space.

"Can I help you? Are you all right?"

I recognize Elliot's voice, but just barely. I've never heard that tone from him before, like he actually gives a damn about his fellow human beings. He's not the kind to waste his concern on people he doesn't care about.

He wouldn't use that tone if he knew it was me standing out here.

"Hello? Can you understand me?" He moves out of the doorway, coming toward me. One hand—a long-fingered, broad-palmed hand—shields his eyes from the rain.

I know I have to say something, but my voice won't work. It's all I can do to hug the hard drive closer to my chest, the edges sharp against my bare skin. I'm more than shivering now—the cold is wracking through me, coming in great, shuddering waves. Like the waves of the water beneath my feet, ready to sweep me away.

There's no safety for me here, no rescue. But I have nowhere else to go.

The light from the entryway illuminates Elliot's face piece by piece. There's concern and worry sketched across his features. He looks painfully human. No one's looked at me like that in years.

Then he sees it's me, and it's all wiped clean.

He stops dead, almost like he's internally slamming on the brakes. His mouth twists in a grimace.

"No." It's all he says. Stark and clear and condemning.

He steps backward into the warmth and light of the doorway, then slams the door.

CHAPTER 2

As the light from the door collapses into a thin wedge, taking my hope with it, my body reacts. My legs push me forward, my feet sailing over the gap between the dock and the deck as if it weren't there, as if I weren't utterly terrified of it.

I grab the door just before it closes, the frame biting into the backs of my fingers. It hurts, but I hold on.

For a moment I think Elliot will smash my fingers in the door. I'm not surprised.

Slowly he pulls the door back open. Rain slides into the entryway, spattering his shirt and sweats.

Wait, he's wearing normal clothes?

He gives the door a jerk, a not-so-nice reminder that I'm still holding on to it. I let go as if burned.

"I need your help." I stare right at him as I say it, looking deep into his eyes. They're blue and icy cold.

He doesn't respond or even react. Not that I should have expected him to. I could be on fire and Elliot probably wouldn't spit on me to put it out.

I squeeze the hard drive case and gather my wits. "I'm the mole," I blurt. "The one Fuchs has been searching for."

My chest tightens as I confess. I've been hiding that for so long, and I just… said it.

He shakes his head. "No, you're not. You're devoted to him."

Not me. Minerva is the one who's devoted to him. But I'm not explaining that to Elliot. There are people I need to protect.

And there's no point arguing with him since he's a lawyer. "I have all the evidence." I reach under my shirt and pull out the hard drive.

Elliot's eyes go wide, and he takes two quick steps toward me, instinctively reaching for the drive. His plain white T-shirt pulls tight across his chest, and his sweatpants shift on his hips, riding dangerously low.

His feet are bare.

That's the detail that snags my attention and doesn't let go. His feet are bare, naked, completely exposed to me. Raindrops collect on his skin, and the floor must be cold against his soles. But he's rock solid, not even flinching, like he doesn't feel the cold at all.

Maybe he doesn't. As for me, I suddenly realize that I'm shivering so hard I'm in danger of dropping the drive.

Elliot notices and reaches for it. His fingers brush the case, but I pull it back and over my head. "No."

He cocks his head, so slowly it's almost a threat. I keep the drive held up high, water dripping off it into my hair and face.

He steps back, holding the door open. "I suppose you better come inside."

I've never received such a grudging invitation, and I'm one of the most hated women in Silicon Valley. But it's still an invitation.

I pull the drive into my chest, and as I curl around it, my muscles seize with cold, locking me into a strange half crouch. Warmth and light and rescue are a few feet away—and I've been invited inside like some kind of vampire—but I can't reach it. I still can't reach it, after all this effort.

He glances back at me, his features stark with irritation. "Come on."

"I can't," I chatter from between clenched teeth. Shame burns through me that he should see me so weak, but it's not enough warmth to unclench my muscles.

With one long arm, he reaches out and snags my elbow, pulling me into the houseboat. As soon as my foot lands inside, he drops his hand like I've burned him. Actually shakes it out, like I'm coated with acid or something and he can't wait to get it off.

"Shoes off," he says, giving me his back.

I kick off my heels, which are filled with water, and leave them by the door. I step onto a plush carpet, my feet sinking gratefully into the warm pile of it.

Even though I'm dripping wet and shivering hard enough to shatter my bones, I can't help but be impressed by his houseboat. Houseboats usually conjure up images of something dingy and dark and from the seventies, when wood paneling was all the rage. But this is airy and modern with touches of coziness throughout. There's a galley kitchen against one wall, a long bench seat piled high with pillows under a long row of windows, and a small dining area. To my left is a set of stairs that presumably lead up to the bedroom. The rain pounds at the windows, the wind screaming around us, but it seems more like a show put on for our entertainment when it's outside this cozy environment.

It's small, yes, but it feels luxuriously small, if that makes any sense. Like a person could happily lock themselves away here for the rest of their life. It's exactly what I could've hoped for in a hiding place and exactly what I didn't expect from him.

I stand in the narrow entry hallway so as not to drip on the rug throughout the rest of the boat. Elliot's definitely the kind of guy who wouldn't appreciate muddy water on his rugs, especially if that muddy water came from me.

Elliot crosses his arms and stares at me. "I don't believe you. I can't tell what you and Fuchs are trying to do here, but it's nothing good. The hard drive as a prop"—he jerks his chin at it, and how can a chin look hot like that?—"was smart though, I'll give you that."

"So why invite me in?"

He sighs heavily. "Because I didn't want you to drown. I'm going to call a car for you; you can go anywhere you want. As long as it's not here."

"I'm not lying."

"You're breathing, which means you are."

That's not fair. While I might have done some evil shit in the service of Fuchs, I never lied. I fired people, destroyed their careers, even their lives, but I never lied. At least not to him.

My breathing goes shallow. It sounds so small, my truthfulness next to everything else I've done.

I wet my lips, shift my grip on the hard drive. "I stole all this from Corvus. It exposes… everything. I know you don't trust me, but I promise it's legitimate."

"You're right," he says slowly. "I don't trust you. So what the hell are you doing here?"

I don't even know how to begin to answer that. Should I begin five years ago, when I decided to go undercover at Corvus and assumed the identity of Minerva to do it?

Or should I start five months ago, when I realized that Fuchs was closing in on me and I should make my escape plan?

Or should I begin a few weeks ago, when I realized that Elliot's hatred would make the perfect cover for when I did flee?

"No one will look for me here." It's the truth, because I've never lied to him.

His eyes narrow. "Did you steal money?"

As if. Money is nothing compared to what I have. Fuchs

has paid me very, very well in the years I've been with him. I spent none of it, so I've several million stashed in a bank account. I can't touch it of course because Fuchs will be able to trace me that way.

"No," I say. "Just documents, programs, internal memos."

"Which you won't let me see." He raises one eyebrow in challenge.

"I didn't steal it for you."

"Then who did you steal it for?"

Humanity. The future. Anyone who could be hurt or even killed by these programs, which is everyone.

It's so stupidly naive that I'd never dare say it to him. "I need to contact some people and hand it over to them."

"So you stole it for another company." Does he sound almost *disappointed* in me? "I hope they're paying you a shit ton of money because you're going to need it when Fuchs comes after you."

"It's not another company. Please, just let me use a computer or a phone. I'll contact my friends and then be out of here."

"Okay, let's play this game." He crosses his arms. "So, I believe that you've stolen documents from Corvus for... some reason. You stay here, where he won't look, contact these mysterious friends, and then disappear. Do I have that right?"

That's exactly my plan, but when he says it like that, I deflate. He must have been a terror in the courtroom, smashing his opposition with that sneer of his. It's the neutron bomb of sneers.

And yet he still looks remarkably handsome. What an asshole.

"Yes," I say, as firmly as I can. My hair is soaked, my clothes are dripping, and I'm covered in goose bumps, so I can't summon that much resolve.

He shakes his head. "Wow, Fuchs must be having a

psychotic break or something. Is this really the plan he came up with to infiltrate the Bastards? And how did you agree to it?"

I close my eyes tight. I'm not crazy, although it felt like I was losing my mind in the beginning, trying to remember that I was Minerva now and not—

"It's not a trick." My voice is as cold as my skin.

"Then show me." His gaze lingers on the hard drive, clutched close to my breasts.

"I can't trust you with this," I whisper.

He laughs, a rusty, hollow sound. "Exactly." He reaches for his phone sitting on a kitchen counter. Most things are only an arm's length away in this place. "I'll call the Uber then."

"Wait." I step so quickly toward him he rears back, as if he instinctively can't stand to be even that close to me.

He's right. I'm expecting him to take me in, trust me, but I can't return the favor. I'll have to show him what's on the drive to buy his trust. To buy some shelter until I can find some real friends, the ones I have from my old life.

I hope what I've stolen is enough to buy his silence too. That he doesn't take what I've gathered and use it for his own ends.

"It doesn't belong to you," I say, slow and deliberate. "You have to understand that." My grip on the drive relaxes slightly.

His gaze is locked on the drive, or maybe my arms around it. My skin sizzles and pops uncomfortably. He nods, once, the slightest inclination of his head.

I swallow, my heart speeding. I have to give the drive to him, let him crack it open, expose all its secrets. I've done a million things harder than this in the past five years. So many things that turned my stomach.

Or at least they would have if I hadn't been too busy being Minerva.

I loosen my arms, inch by inch. The drive slips down,

settling against my stomach. If I let go any more, it will fall to the floor. I have to take it in my hand, give it over to him. He's only an arm's length away, like everything else here.

Minerva would shove it right into his chest, which is what I do.

He catches it without surprise, which infuriates me. He should have the decency to be caught off guard by me. His big hands close around the drive, gentle as if it were a kitten.

I'm left with nothing but my wet clothes and my shivers, which are stealing my breath while my fingers, toes, and ears go numb. There's a faint drip, drip, drip at my feet, muddy water making its way from the hem of my coat to the rug.

I want to cry. Minerva would never cry, not for anything, but me…

"Go ahead." I say it as defiantly as I could ever hope for, my courage rushing back. "Go look. I know you want to."

He turns the drive this way and that, like he could see inside it if he just looked hard enough. My chest—he was looking at it exactly like that.

I fold my arms over my breasts, hug myself hard. Partly to get warm—although it feels like that will never happen again, I'm so wet and cold and partly to hide from him, even a little. Without my armor of being Minerva Dyne, enforcer for one of the most powerful men in the world, I'm realizing how big, how suspicious Elliot is.

The drive turns and turns in his hands. I'll have to sit here, cold and wet, humiliated, ignored, while he looks through it. It will be on purpose too, to show me just how unwanted I am. To bring me as low as he thinks I deserve.

Elliot looks at the drive, then looks at me. Then once more at the drive and back at me, as if weighing what I'm worth compared to the information on the drive.

The drive hits the kitchen counter with a thunk that makes me jump. Elliot is staring at me, not the drive. "You need fresh clothes. A warm shower. Come on."

It's not kindness, not when it comes so grudgingly. But I have to take it.

"What about the data?" I stay right where I am, wanting to grab the drive and take it with me. But I get the sense that if I do that, this tentative peace will be shattered.

Cease-fire. That's what this is. It's way too tense to be a *peace.*

"I'll look while you're upstairs. Come on."

He starts up the steps, the set of his shoulders telling me I'm not going to get another chance.

I have no clothes that will fit her.

I don't stop rummaging through my drawers though, searching in vain for what I know won't be there. The house-boat doesn't have storage for anything besides my clothes, and I don't keep things for guests. My one-night stands are just that—one night, nothing permanent, not even a tooth-brush for them to use once and toss.

She can't stay in my home, in spite of all her talk about how no one will look for her here. When I touched her elbow, there was a flare of... Fuck, I don't know. Heat and sparks, equal parts anger and attraction. If I hadn't let go of her immediately, I don't know what would have happened.

My hand is still tingling.

Minerva Dyne is not a woman I can trust. I don't believe her about being the mole or stealing incriminating docu-ments from Corvus or being safe here. If she knew what she inspires in me, she'd run right back into the storm.

She's harmed the women my brothers love. Which means she's harmed my brothers. Which means I hate her.

But I also want to fuck her. Wanted to from the very first moment I saw her.

I grab a T-shirt and some pajama pants. They're much

too big for her, but she'll have to deal with it. I'll dry her clothes in the small dryer next to the kitchen, then put her in an Uber and wave goodbye. Let someone else deal with her lies.

When I turn to face her, she jerks upright, like I've scared her awake. But it's an act. Minerva would never fall asleep unwillingly. She might not sleep at all.

She pushes her hair out of her eyes, her fingers red with cold. Christ, she really needs a hot shower.

I don't want her here, in my most private space. But I also don't want her to freeze to death.

"Come here." The brusqueness of my tone has her jumping. "You need a shower. You'll never warm up otherwise."

She grabs her shirt front as if she's a virgin maiden and I'm a medieval warrior bent on ravishing her. Again, it's an act. Minerva eats men for breakfast, not the other way around.

"I… I know." But she doesn't move toward the bathroom door.

I cross my arms. "Look, why come to me if you're"—I swallow hard, my conscience pricking me even though this woman doesn't even have one—"afraid of me? Isn't there anyone else you could go to?"

She shrugs, a sharp, dismissive gesture. "I know how his mind works."

When she does that, her shirt gapes, revealing a long triangle of smooth skin. I've never allowed her skin—or any other part of her—to feature in my fantasies, but that glimpse is going to haunt me.

She goes on. "He knows you hate me—all the Bastards do, but you personally, especially—so this will be the last place he'll look."

This is the point where I should be polite, should tell her that of course I don't hate her. That it's wrong to hate anyone. It's what my mother would always say, even when my father was doing his worst to bring our family into ruin. I don't hate him. It's wrong to hate.

Well, I hated my father. I understand that I don't interact with people the way others do, that I don't always see the need for the rules that govern social interactions, but I still understand the rules.

The rule about hating I've never really understood though. My father spent us into poverty, put the gray in my mother's hair, and added to the stress that stripped the flesh from her bones. Shouldn't she have hated him? I certainly did.

I don't say anything to Minerva. I don't owe her any polite lies. "Get in the shower."

Her head snaps up at my curt offer. She opens her mouth on a weak, polite refusal.

"Don't argue."

For a moment the defiant, arrogant light in her eyes is very much like the old Minerva. And then it dies. "Fine."

That's not acceptance—that's defeat. I feel like an asshole suddenly, more than I usually do. But goddamn it, she can't appear here in the middle of a rainstorm with supposedly stolen data and expect me to believe her. Even if she did give me the drive to look over.

"This way." I open the bathroom door, move aside so she can enter. My body hits high-alert status when she comes close to the bed. She's my enemy, and I've let her into my den.

She's also my fantasy, my dark and twisted one, and I've got her within inches of my bed.

I don't worry that I'll do something stupid—I've never in my life done anything impulsive—but I do take a moment to tamp down my response. Bury, bury, bury—it's the best way to handle any unwanted thoughts.

I set the clothes on the bed. "There are towels in the cabinet."

She's looking very carefully at the floor, tensed as if I'm going to grab her. Or worse. "Thank you."

I say nothing as I go down the stairs. I don't want her thanks. I don't want her here at all.

I make myself a cup of coffee, listening to her upstairs. The walls are thin, so I hear every rustle, every gentle thunk. I don't imagine her naked. Bury, bury, bury every single hint of those thoughts.

When the shower starts, I reach for my laptop. Finn would have a fit if he saw what I'm about to do, but he's not here. And I can't resist my curiosity.

I plug the hard drive into my laptop. The drive whirs into life, an icon popping up on my laptop screen. Finn would tell me not to open the drive on my machine in case Minerva's loaded this thing with some virus.

But if there is a virus that's going to smoke my computer, I can always get a new one. And I'll know that Minerva's been bullshitting me and I can throw her out with a clean conscience.

I double-click the icon, and a folder pops up on my screen. The file names make no sense to me, not that I've got the programming knowledge to understand them. I'm a lawyer—my brother is the coder.

But my computer hasn't melted down. So probably no viruses.

There are some PDFs and text files there. I open those since they ought to be in English, which I do understand.

The first few are software schematics, describing things I don't understand or care about. The rest of the Bastards will go crazy for this—assuming Minerva isn't giving us fake shit —but it means nothing to me.

The next few are much more interesting. One's on NSA letterhead, another is plain text but is clearly written by someone working for a government intelligence agency. And the other one...

I read it once quickly, then again slowly. I understand it—of course I do, it's signed by the attorney general of the United States himself—but I can't quite believe it.

If this is real… If this is real, Minerva is in danger from more than just Corvus. Way more danger.

CHAPTER 4

The clothes don't fit, but I never expected them to.

When I slip the shirt over my head, it falls to midthigh, the collar sagging perilously close to my nipples. I tug the collar up, but there's still too much of my chest on display, the swell of my breasts way too prominent for my peace of mind.

And then there're my nipples—without my bra, they're hard and full, the cotton agonizingly soft as it rubs against them. But I left my bra hanging to dry in the bathroom; it's too wet to put back on.

The pants are a little better—everything that should be hidden by them is—but the excess fabric pools around my feet, waiting for me to trip over it.

I push my wet hair back from my face. There was a comb sitting on the sink, but I didn't dare use it. It's his comb, and it's bad enough that I'm in his house, using his shower, wearing his clothes; I want to limit my contact with his things as much as possible.

He hates me. I wrap my arms around myself to hold in my shiver. He's made it very, very clear that he doesn't buy my story. That he'll take any excuse to kick me out.

I wasn't expecting him to believe me right away, but being

this close to him and feeling that hate in such a visceral way is affecting me more than I expected. It's one thing to face down that cold look of his across a boardroom. It's something much sharper, more deadly, to face it in this tiny houseboat.

I tug the pants up, but the second I let go, they slip back down. There's nothing much more I can do to make myself presentable. So now I have to go face the lion in his den.

I move slowly down the stairs, my limbs achy with the cold. The shower warmed me up some, but not quite enough. I wonder if I'll ever get warm again.

The steps are of some dark hardwood, gleaming and waxed and smooth and cool beneath my feet. It's almost as luxurious as the carpet.

He's sitting at the small dining table, his laptop out and the hard drive plugged into it. He doesn't see me as I come in, giving me a moment to study him.

I can tell from the intense focus on his face he's going through the files. That's exactly what I hoped he would do—see the proof and finally believe me—but I still feel a surge of possessiveness, of sour jealousy. I gave my life for those files, spent five years collecting and hiding all of them, and he's just scrolling through them, obscenely available to him. Easy.

I have to get used to the sensation. If all goes to plan, the entire world will read those files. My life will probably be ruined in the process, but after five years undercover, I don't have much of a life to go back to.

I wrap my arms around myself, slipping into Minerva mode to hold back my sadness.

Elliot still hasn't noticed me. His expression is stern, focused, but not angry. He looks almost… well, almost inviting. I realize that's because this is the very first time I've seen him not angry. He still looks like he's no picnic, but definitely more manageable.

I could get used to the way he looks now.

He lifts his head, catches me watching. "How did you manage to get yourself caught in a turf war between the CIA and the NSA?"

So he went right to the juicy bits. He's smart, deadly smart, so of course he would.

"Elements of each," I say, correcting him. "I don't think the entire agency on either side is behind this. Only certain factions want the Corvus plan."

Elliot rubs a hand over his face. "This is pretty explosive stuff."

He's struggling with it, I can tell. But then it's a lot to wrestle with.

To explain the size of what Elliot's trying to grapple with, we have to go back to the beginning, back when the CIA was first founded. They were meant to only spy on people outside the country—any operations within the country were strictly forbidden. At least, that's how the story goes.

Now we bring in the NSA. They're signals intelligence, monitoring enemy transmissions, cracking encryption codes, things like that. They're not supposed to collect or listen in on American citizens without a warrant. At least, that's how the story goes.

My boss, Arne Fuchs, has developed the technology to allow someone to grab almost every single electronic transmission in the United States—every phone call, text message, email, direct message, all of it—and the machine-learning algorithms to go through all those masses of messages, looking for anything that the CIA or the NSA would want to see.

Selling that program to a government agency would make billions for Corvus. But it's not the money Fuchs wants: it's the information. All those messages would have to get processed through Corvus servers, and Fuchs put in a back door so that he could get a look as that information passed through.

Certain people within the CIA and the NSA loved the program—code-named OmniView—so much that they didn't care that it was illegal. The prospect of all that intelligence was simply too enticing. And of course the CIA didn't want the NSA to have it and vice versa. Never mind that they're supposed to be working together to keep Americans safe from foreign threats; holding tight to their own patch of power is much more important to those factions.

So they're fighting within their respective agencies to acquire and use OmniView and with anyone outside their agency to make sure only they get the wonderful toys they want so badly.

I don't need to explain all the legal implications of that to Elliot. He knows OmniView is completely illegal and that if I blow the whistle and expose it, I'll go to jail. Probably for a very, very long time.

My best bet is to release the information to a news source as anonymously as I can, then flee the country and spend the rest of my life in hiding. It's not a great plan—Fuchs is going to know it was me, and he'll be sure to pass that on to the government—but my own safety was probably always forfeit. It's the information that matters. I just have to stay alive long enough to get it to the right people.

"So you believe me now?" I ask quietly.

He doesn't say yes, but he also doesn't say no. "This is so fucked."

I agree. "Are you going to turn me in?"

His jaw works. He's angry again. "This all could be faked."

"Why would I do that?"

He turns his head as if searching for a reason. He exhales slow and hard when he can't find one. "I won't turn you in."

But he won't say if he believes me or not. I suppose I should be happy just for this.

"Will you tell anyone?" I ask.

He glances up at me over his shoulder, his dark eyes searing.

"You're a lawyer," I say quickly. "Is everything we say protected by attorney-client privilege?"

His expression is sardonic. "You're not my client." Implied is the notion that no amount of money would ever persuade him to work for me.

"I can't take this to just anyone," I say quietly. "If Fuchs finds me... or the NSA or the CIA..."

He nods grimly. "Yes, I can see your dilemma. Don't worry, I'm not going to throw you out. Not yet." He lifts his hands, gestures at the laptop. "I have no idea where to begin with this."

I have some ideas. First I need to get ahold of my old friends, tell them I'm finally out. Maybe make some copies of the drive and put them in safe places should anything happen to me.

Next, I'm going to contact some people I know in the media. Most of the reporters I know work for fringe websites, the kind nobody takes seriously, even though they're the only ones speaking the truth about the surveillance state. They can help me contact others in the media and make sure this gets spread far and wide. That's the only hope to stop it.

Problem is, once Fuchs discovers my real name—and he will, given enough time—he'll track down anyone I've ever even had coffee with and interrogate them. The people from my old life could easily lead Fuchs right to me.

Fuchs has a noose around my neck. I only have a certain amount of time before he starts to tighten it, and I've got to release this data before then.

After... Well, I can't think about after.

"I told you," I say. "I need to contact some people. And then I can leave."

"Like who?"

"I can't tell you. You wouldn't know them anyway."

"Right. And they can't be googled?"

"They can, which is the problem." I cross my arms, mirroring his combative stance. "I'm not telling you their names. That's nonnegotiable."

He doesn't smile, but he does look amused. "And you've got the leverage to demand anything." Meaning that of course I don't.

I may not have leverage, but I'm stubborn. Minerva doesn't bend for anyone, no matter how desperate she is.

"No." I keep still and steady, staring straight into his eyes. "That's not happening."

We stare each other down for several heartbeats. The air between us grows heavy, almost sluggish in my lungs. I can see the slight imperfections in him—nose tip a bit too sharp, the dent in his chin a touch too deep, his mouth turned down and the lines around it saying that's how he always holds it.

He breaks it off first, and I feel a hint of triumph. I might not have *leverage*, but I can still beat him in a staring contest.

"Why don't you start from beginning?" He gestures to the bench seat across from him.

I simply stand there for a moment. The beginning of what? When I became an activist? When I started at Corvus? Or when I decided it was finally time to get out of there?

I sit down, carefully rearranging my clothes—*his* clothes. I don't want to expose any more of my body than necessary. As I adjust my legs, my knee brushes his and sends shivers through me. I tuck my legs as close to my body as I can, trying to make myself small.

His mouth twists with pained amusement when he sees what I'm doing. "Don't worry, I won't touch you." His tone says he'd rather cut off his hand than do that.

I wish I could say the feeling was mutual, but it's not.

"Which part of the beginning?" I ask. I'm not going to tell

him everything. He's wily enough to track down my friends if I give too much away.

He spreads his hands to encompass the computer and the hard drive. "How did we end up here? All this time we thought you were Fuchs's lapdog. His happy little lieutenant. It turns out you were fooling us all along."

I suppose I can start a few months ago, when Fuchs began to suspect there was a double agent in his operation. Someone—me—leaked some information to Finn Braden, who's a partner at Bastard Capital like Elliot. It was a risk, and I knew Fuchs would start sniffing around if I did it, but innocent people were going to jail. I couldn't take it anymore.

Funny, the things that will finally push a person over the edge. I'd done a lot worse things for Fuchs, things that should have made me throw up just to think about, but I hadn't even blinked. Minerva wouldn't have blinked, so I didn't.

"I couldn't take it anymore." I say it as plain and simple as it was. At least for that particular act of sabotage.

He snorts. "Corvus put spyware on everyone's phones, without their knowledge. Weren't you involved in that?"

"I wrote the terms for the social media apps that let us do that." I don't blink as I say it.

"Fuchs was also secretly running that gossip blog, the one that was trying to break up my brother's marriage. I'm sure you were intimately involved in that too."

"I told him to buy the site," I say. "And I suggested planting those stories about your brother's infidelity."

He looks away, his mouth tightening. But only for a moment, and then he's pinned me with those dark blue eyes again. "And the panopticon? That whole system Corvus came up with to put whoever they wanted in jail? Like mentally ill homeless men? What'd you do for that one?"

If he thinks listing my crimes is going to break me, he's very mistaken. I do this every night, remind myself of all the terrible, inhumane shit I've unleashed on this world. It's the only way I can keep in touch with who I was before, the woman buried deep beneath Minerva.

Elliot's prosecutor role-play is lost on me. I'm the ultimate actress, the ultimate liar.

"I negotiated with the police department, set up liaisons with the prosecutor's office, even mapped out where all the cameras should be." My tone is as cold and smooth as ice. Not even a hint of dark shame in the crystal of it.

He leans back, his mouth cracking open. "Jesus, you just admitted to it all. Like you're proud of it."

Not quite, but I don't deny it. I did what I had to, and I don't have to explain myself to him. I'm not going to beg for his approval.

"I'm not denying any of it. It's public record."

"Not all of it," he counters. "So after all this… evil shit, you just decide, 'Hey, I've realized I'm a blight on humanity! Time to quit this job.'"

I shouldn't let it, but that jab about being a blight on humanity hurts. A lot.

He leans in close, points his long forefinger at me. "Or, more likely, you've been selling information to other companies, realized you were about to get caught, and decided to try to save your skin here. Make yourself look like some kind of noble whistle-blower."

It's a lovely story except for one thing. "Then why would I give all that information to Finn Braden for free?"

He drops his finger, a nasty smile crossing his mouth. "So you admit you were the leak?"

I take a deep breath and resist the urge to slam my hand on the table. "That's what I said from the moment I walked in. You didn't get me on anything."

"But if I keep pushing, I will." The naked resentment in his voice turns my stomach.

I've given him everything I have—at least, everything on

the hard drive—but he still hates me. Despises me. Which I should have guessed that he wouldn't magically forgive me. None of this was going to be easy.

"Go ahead and try me." It feels good to challenge him. He might be my only hope here, but he's still an arrogant ass.

He gathers himself up, bristling for a fight, and my pulse surges. I bristle myself, ready to leap at him. With arguments, not physically, of course.

Then he sits back, his intensity fading. "It's two in the morning. You need to sleep."

I want to protest, if only to push back against him, but he's right. I'm fading and fast.

I rise from the bench and he does too, in some parody of chivalry. "I'll take the couch," I say. "If you have any blankets…?"

He shakes his head like I'm just too funny. "Nope. You're in my bed."

I freeze. But I'm also wicked hot suddenly, heat blooming under my skin. Every inch of it.

"I won't be in there with you," he says. The expression on his face makes me want to punch him. "I'll take the couch."

"No, really—"

"That way you can't sneak out without my knowing."

I shut my mouth hard enough to have my jaws clacking. Right. Because I'm a sneak and a villain and I can't be trusted.

I've brought this all on myself, but it still hurts.

CHAPTER 5

"You have got to be fucking with me." My brother Logan is in my kitchen, a mug of coffee in his hand and a stunned expression on his face. "She's *upstairs*? Right now?"

I nod, trying to signal with my closed mouth that he needs to keep it down. He's going to wake up Minerva, and I don't want that to happen. Yet.

"Is that the hard drive?" Logan reaches for it. "Holy shit, I can't believe it."

I grab his hand. "I can't let you look at it," I say apologetically.

Logan doesn't care about my apology, only about the prize so close at hand. "You're kidding. You're really not going to let me look at it?"

I shake my head. "It's… technically it is still hers."

"But you looked at it."

I blackmailed her into it though, which feels… dirty right now. I had to do it of course, to make sure she was telling the truth, but reminding myself of that doesn't help.

"I did, but you'll just have to take my word that it's explosive. She really is in deep shit."

Logan scoffs. "If she is—which I don't believe—it's her own damn fault. This is Minerva, remember? She doesn't need any help from us. She definitely doesn't need protecting."

"Honey." Callie lays a soft hand on his arm. "I'm sure Elliot has his reasons." But her expression says she doesn't understand either.

I'm not sure I do myself.

"I just can't see her having a change of heart," Logan says. "Or even possessing a heart. And I can't see you falling for it."

I shift, my feet scraping over the bare floor. I'm near the doorway, where Minerva came in last night, cold and dripping. I told Logan how she looked, but without seeing it for himself, he doesn't believe me. He didn't see the fear in her eyes, how… undone she was. He's only ever seen Minerva pulled together, so tight she's unbreakable. He can't imagine what I saw.

"Why come last night then?" I argue. "With only a hard drive, soaked to the skin?" I refuse to linger in my thoughts about her skin. "If she wanted to sell this data, she could have done it easily from the comfort of her own place, not walked through a rainstorm to me."

"Assuming she has a home and doesn't plug into the wall in Fuchs's office at night." Logan shakes his head. "You're only arguing about this because that's what you do for a living. You argue. You don't believe her any more than we do. But fine, you want to argue, we'll argue. First point, why now? Fuchs has been doing terrible shit forever. What's changed for her?"

I don't have a good answer to that one.

"Sometimes people just… break," Callie says. "There's no one thing. They just decide they've had enough."

Logan's face is stark with painful memories. Callie left him a while back, fed up with how their marriage was falling apart. She just left, without a word, breaking his heart in the process.

That's hard for me to forget and even harder for me to

forgive. Seeing Logan in those months… it still haunts me. They might be reconciled now and happier than ever, but that period of their relationship can never be erased.

"What happened…," he says in a rough voice. "Our separation was partly her fault. She was spying on you, that's why she swooped in when she thought we were divorcing. Like a vulture come to pick over a carcass."

I pinch the bridge of my nose. I was hoping just Logan would come over this morning, without Callie. She and Minerva have a history, and while Callie and I don't quite get along, I don't want to rub her nose in Minerva's presence.

"I know." Callie's holding back tears. "But we're okay now."

I sigh. "I know all that. I remember each and every awful, shitty thing she did. But she's here now, and I need to do something about it."

"And that's why you called us, to help kick her out." Logan's chin juts forward. "Although you should have called some priests to perform an exorcism. First, though, we should go through her drive."

"Look, I asked you over to help me figure out what to do with her," I say. "Not go through her hard drive. It's off the table, and that's final."

"Okay. Well, here's my advice: get rid of her. Don't listen to any more of her lies; don't look at whatever fake shit is on that drive. Nothing that comes out of her mouth is real." Logan's grip on the mug tightens. "After what she did to Callie…"

His wife's hand on his arm clenches, her mouth going white.

"It's okay," Callie says quietly. "I'm not afraid of her."

Logan takes her hand, kisses her knuckles. "There's nothing to be afraid of. Because Elliot's going to show her the door."

My jaw goes rigid. Logan is the oldest, and sometimes he

seems to forget I'm not a little kid anymore. That I don't need to be told what to do.

I pick up the drive. "What's on here is explosive. And no, I won't show it to you since I don't have permission. If we do the same shit they do, doesn't that make us as bad as they are?"

"Aren't lawyers supposed to be amoral bloodsuckers?" Logan asks wryly.

"I think I missed that day in class." I didn't, since I had perfect attendance in law school, but I know what he means. I can bend the law to my will in a million different ways, not all of them... well, moral, I guess. But I've never been unethical, and it's not my fault ethics and morals aren't the same thing.

The question is, Is showing them the drive a violation of my ethics or my morals? And what do I owe to someone who deserves only the sharp side of justice?

"She wants to contact some people from here," I say. "She wouldn't say who. But then she guarantees she'll be gone."

"To sell this data to someone?" Logan sneers at the drive. "How do you even know it's real? Let me look, help you decide."

Callie sinks down into one of the chairs in the living room, the canal glittering behind her through the windows. The rain is gone, although the sky remains gray, and the streets are littered with everything the wind picked up and dropped. Still, it's a pretty scene.

"Maybe we should leave aside the question of whether or not it's real," she says. She puts a hand on her rounded belly, almost unconsciously. "What would she have to gain by selling this information? Fuchs could still have her prosecuted."

A chill runs over me because the people she's supposedly on the run from would do much worse than that. "It's beyond that," I say. "If it is real, we're—she's dealing with much bigger forces than a prosecutor's office."

I don't need to detail for them who that might be. They know Corvus's biggest clients as well as I do.

Logan sets down his mug, his mouth slack. "Well, it should be her problem. Not yours." But he doesn't sound so certain now.

"You could go to jail too, right?" Callie asks. "If you help her and the government comes after her."

"Possibly." I stare at the floor, my mind going through the defenses I might use. "There is attorney-client privilege. Even the worst people in the world are entitled to legal advice."

"She's not your client." Logan gestures angrily. "Come on, don't involve yourself in this. Tell her to fuck off. It's what she'd have done to you."

"Hello."

Minerva's soft voice from the top of the stairs has all of us going rigid. I don't know how much she's heard, but even Logan's last few words were more than enough.

She comes down, still in my T-shirt and sweats, her feet bare. Her dark brown hair hangs around her shoulders. I've never seen it like that before, loose and dry and looking oh so soft.

"He's right." She stops on the last step and crosses her arms as she stares at us. "I wouldn't have helped you. Before."

When her gaze falls on Callie, her cheeks go pink, then red, and her gaze cuts away. Guilt comes off her in waves until she gets her expression back under control. But her cheeks keep their color.

I couldn't sleep last night, and not only because the couch is too damn small to sleep on. She was upstairs, in my house, in my bed. Only a few feet away. My hyperawareness of her was because of what she'd done, how much I loathed her—

but there was also something more there. Something I wish wasn't.

And then there was the hard drive, sitting next to my laptop, a silent black box that held a bomb. I have no idea what to do with the information she's brought, even though I spent most of last night thinking about it, running over all the various legal issues in my head.

None of them came out well for her.

Logan's expression remains angry even in the face of Minerva's guilt. But my brother doesn't really forgive and forget, especially when it comes to Callie.

I also don't forgive and forget, especially when it comes to my brother's wife, which is why Callie and I aren't exactly friendly. I can't forget how badly she hurt my brother, and even though they've reconciled now, forgiveness is hard. I'm trying though.

"At least you admit it," Logan says. "So why should we help you?"

Minerva's eyebrows jerk up. "*We?* I don't remember asking you for anything."

Callie claps her hand over her mouth in shock. "Oh my God. You haven't changed at all."

Minerva shakes her head. "No, I'm still the same old Minerva even if I have left Fuchs." Her gaze cuts to me. "What did you tell them? Everything?"

She doesn't look betrayed… more like she expects me to dump all her secrets out before my brother. Like it's only what she deserves.

It is, of course. So why the hell didn't I do it?

"He didn't tell us anything." Logan's mouth is flat. "Something about professional ethics."

"We're discussing if I should allow you to contact your friends from here," I say, not wanting her to think I'm on her side. My holding back isn't that at all.

"And the verdict?"

"We haven't reached one yet," Callie says softly. "Do you… do you need some clothes? I can go—"

Minerva shakes her head so sharply Callie flinches. "No. I don't want any of the cameras to see you bringing things in here. Like women's clothes."

"Cameras?" Logan scrubs a hand over his face. "Jesus."

Minerva mapped out those cameras—they're all there because of her. It's a good reminder that she's no innocent. Not a bit.

"You can email one person," I say. "Just one, and I want to see the message and the email you're sending it to. That's the only offer you're getting."

Her expression never flickers. It's almost as if the woman I met last night was a mirage, a figment of my imagination. There's not even a hint of give in the woman before me. "And if they don't respond?"

I shrug. "You have three days. If they contact you by then, good for you. If not…"

I look meaningfully at the drive. I wouldn't take it from her—at least I'm not planning to—but I won't hesitate to fight dirty with her.

Minerva doesn't accept or reject my offer. She simply watches me as if measuring my resolve.

Logan, impatient as always, breaks in. "You haven't explained why you came here of all places. Why not straight to this friend? Or even a hotel?"

Minerva keeps her gaze on me. "He watches the hotels. All of them. I guarantee you, Fuchs is searching every hotel in this city and in a hundred-mile radius. He'd find me in an instant."

"But not here?" Logan is deeply skeptical.

"He'd never look for me at Elliot's," she says. "Not in a million years."

"He also wouldn't look for you at our house." Callie makes the offer in a reluctant tone. "And there's more space there. You wouldn't even have to see us."

Callie clearly does not want to see Minerva, not here, not in her house, but she has to make the offer.

It's a kind thing to do, and I haven't always been kind to Callie.

"Don't worry about it," I say gruffly. "You guys have enough to worry about with the baby. It's only three days."

Logan sends me a grateful look.

"Besides," I say, "I want to go through this hard drive more."

There's a flicker of surprise in Minerva's gaze. She thought that one little peek was going to be enough for me. Well, if she's going to stay here, she's going to pay, one way or another.

"Can we see it?" Logan tosses the question offhand, but Minerva isn't fooled.

"No," she says coolly.

"But Elliot got to?"

She doesn't respond to that. "Fine. I agree to your terms, not that I have much choice."

"You always had the choice to walk away," I remind her. She could grab her drive and be out the door in seconds and never see any of us again.

The look she sends me is both defiant and pained. "I never had that choice."

CHAPTER 6

I breathe a sigh of relief once Logan and Callie are gone. Just a small one since Elliot is here, large and looming and way too much physically, but at least I feel less guilty around him.

What I did to Callie, I had to do. Fuchs right to my face told me to find the biggest, most expensive bouquet I could and deliver it to Callie along with his congratulations on the worst day of her life.

Was I trembling, deep inside, when I did? When I shoved those flowers into her arms and sneered at her? Did I feel *any* sympathy? After all, her secret identity had just been exposed and in the most humiliating way possible. It was my darkest fear come to light.

I don't think I did any of those things. All I can remember was how steady my hands were when I passed her the flowers, how I made my tone so perfectly tart, so fake cheery, and how pleased I was that Fuchs would be pleased.

That was it.

Elliot shuts the door behind them, taking a moment to stand there with his hand on the knob. He convinced them to leave again, saying that he'd be just fine alone with me. That I wasn't likely to knife him or anything.

I heard everything they said downstairs, from their greetings all the way to Logan advising Elliot to tell me to fuck off. I can't say I was surprised Elliot called in his brother—I was only surprised he didn't call in all the Bastards. They stick together very tightly, which Fuchs discovered to his eternal fury.

But I still hesitated to confront them. Partly because I was feeling guilty—a strange thing to feel after five years of numbness, like an arm or a leg or my entire body was aflame with pins and needles as sensation flooded back through me —and partly because I wanted to see what Elliot would do. The drive was sitting down there, under his watchful eye, no password protection on it. He could have done anything he wanted with it.

He protected my secrets. That was the biggest surprise of all. He's horribly uptight, so maybe it was just a flicker of conscience or ethics or something that stopped him... but the gesture mattered to me. He's not on my side, but it felt like he might have been in those few moments.

"So?" He turns from the door, pins me with a hard look. "Ready to write that email?"

The sooner that's done, the sooner I can be out of here. I'm astonished he gave me three days. I was expecting a countdown of hours, with me getting tossed in the canal once it reached zero.

I grab the waistband of the sweatpants, pulling them up so I don't trip. "Sure."

I'm actually not. There were four of us at the beginning of this, but I've had no contact with the other three for years, for obvious reasons. Once I was in at Corvus, I couldn't be talking with people from my old life and blowing my cover.

I have their old emails, phone numbers, but I have no idea if they still work. These people aren't on social media, which makes them harder to track down. Face-to-face in the open, without cameras or microphones, is the way they prefer to do things. It's safest.

I sit down in front of his laptop. "Is this machine running the encryption program?"

"You mean the one January had to design to stop your boss? Yes."

Arne had been so furious when that program had been released. The spyware he'd put on everyone's phones hadn't been exposed, at least not publicly, but Pixio putting the encryption on their phones basically rendered the spyware useless. I'd been sent off to limit the damage and punish those Fuchs held responsible.

January is now dating Mark Taylor, who's another Bastard. And one of the people I had to punish was Grace Li —she's currently not allowed into the country. But she's also engaged to Paul Tsai, also a Bastard, so she seems to be doing just fine.

And then there's Ramona Blythe. I put her brother in jail, although I didn't know he was her brother when I did it. She's also dating a Bastard—Finn Braden, who released a virus into Corvus that destroyed a very valuable surveillance program we were going to sell to every police department in the country. And several national governments.

I gave them the information they needed to get that virus into Corvus, although they didn't know it was me. I don't think that's enough for any of them to forgive me, and why should they? The things I did to them are unforgivable.

All I ever did to Elliot was sneer at his legal abilities, and he can't stand to even look at me. The rest of them are going to be ready to carve me up.

And Fuchs... he'll have the cruelest, coldest punishments waiting for me if he ever finds me.

"Good," is all I say as I try to hide all these thoughts running through me. "I don't want this intercepted."

In a few minutes, I've set up a burner account on a faraway server, routing a throwaway email address through a maze of computers, the better to hide where it's coming from. I'm a little rusty since I haven't written any real code in a while. Fuchs has a ton of talented programmers; he never needed me for that.

"There." I open a new email message. "Do you want to watch over my shoulder? Just in case?"

Elliot frowns. He doesn't like being teased, although I suppose I'm being too mean to be truly teasing. "I don't trust you."

As if I need to be told. "That's why I asked if you wanted to watch."

Whoa, that sounds much dirtier than I meant. Any level of dirty with this man is not appropriate, and that was several levels of it.

I duck my head and start typing away, not waiting for him. If he wants to watch, he knows where I am. And thank God I didn't say that aloud.

There's no space for him to loom behind me though—I'm sitting with my back to the wall. He'll have to slide into the bench across from me... or slide next to me.

My eyes never leave the screen, but I feel him move. The air shifts and slips over my skin, warmed by him. The hair near my cheek stirs, whispers across my face like a caress.

And then he's motioning me over and sitting right next to me, arm to arm, thigh to thigh. There's space of course—it might be a booth, but it's a luxurious one—except Elliot redefines space. What should be ample becomes *not enough* and *too much.*

It's because he's so tall and his shoulders are so broad, and I have to stop thinking about this. I've stopped typing because it feels like he's stealing all the oxygen. Oh, and my brain has stopped working.

Minerva would never fall for this. But I don't feel like her right now.

"I'm writing to a friend," I say. "One I can trust." I point to the screen, although all there is to see is the email address.

But he's making a mental note of it, and he's definitely going to search out everything he can about it. I wouldn't expect anything less from him.

My fingers hover over the keys since I can't think of what to write. Or at least how to put it in a code she'll understand without revealing anything to anyone who might intercept this. I've decided to try my one email on Deena. She was the steadiest of all of us, besides me. That's why we decided I was the one who'd go undercover—I was the one who wouldn't break.

Elliot jerks his chin at the laptop as if to say *Get on with it.* His scent hits me as he does.

I can't help my deep, appreciative inhale. He didn't change his sheets before I crawled into them. I don't think he even thought of it. The linen smelled of soap and musk, exactly like he smells sitting next to me. I dreamed of that scent—I was bathing in it, in his shower, in the dream. It was the best shower of my life.

This doesn't feel like the best moment of my life though, with him so close and my stomach in a double knot. My pulse is vibrating sickeningly through my fingers, making them want to tremble.

I pull air in through my nose, flex my fingers. *I'm out* appears in the message window. *Need a meeting place. Here— have no transportation. And soon.*

It's short, blunt, almost like what a man would write. All the better to hide my identity, although I wrote emails almost as curt as this when I was at Corvus. Something like that from a superior, one who was at the right hand of God like I was, and a woman too, scared people. They'd think they were in trouble somehow. And I used that fear to my advantage.

Elliot shifts next to me, the table vibrating under my elbows as he does. "That's it?"

"Does it pass inspection?"

"It seems short. How will they know it's you?"

Five years is a long time. I've almost forgotten who I used to be, which doesn't bode well for Deena remembering.

"She'll know," I say.

"She?" He pounces like a cat on a bug.

Shit. I didn't mean to give that away. "Or he," I lie. "I'm not sure which of them will see this email first."

"So there's several of you? In whatever scheme this is?"

I determinedly don't meet his eyes. This interrogation wasn't part of the bargain. "Is the email okay? Can I hit Send?"

There's a beat where I sense him preparing another question, maybe a whole series of them. "If you want to waste your one shot on that, go ahead. Although you could have just gone to the library to send that."

My skin crawls as I remember just how many cameras Corvus installed in and around every branch of the San Francisco Public Library. Civic-minded people go to the library, groups congregate there to plan to make the world better. Of course Fuchs would want to keep an extra close eye on that.

"Fine." I hit Send, and in an instant the email is gone, fluttering through the ether like a sparrow made of ones and zeros.

I wait for Elliot to move, to let me out, but he doesn't. I could elbow him, but that would require physical contact. Bad idea.

"You worked for Fuchs for five years."

"You googled me. I'm flattered."

"Before that, you worked at a chip maker. And before that, a mobile phone manufacturer. Nothing exciting or splashy. All very middle-of-the-road, stodgy companies."

He's searching for something, but I'm not sure what. I actually didn't do any of those things—we seeded the internet with fake facts about Minerva, an employee profile here, a LinkedIn connection there. Enough to make Minerva real but not enough for anyone to get suspicious about. She wasn't supposed to stand out because Fuchs doesn't want anyone in his company to attract attention.

"Right." I drum my fingers on the table as if I'm impatient to end this. "And before that, a computer science degree from UCSD." Not a great school but a good-enough one. Again, exactly what Fuchs was looking for, even though he went to Stanford.

And again, that was not what I'd actually done. I started a CS degree at Berkeley, then dropped out with a year to go. There hadn't seemed much point in finishing, not when I was learning so much more in the real world.

I bet if I told Elliot I'm a college dropout, he'd faint dead away. He probably thinks anything less than the Ivy League is slumming it.

"I'm just trying to put the pieces of you together in my head," he says. It's not a kind or even curious tone. He sounds like he's going to disassemble me as soon as he can after. "Where do these friends come in? And what in you made you leave in the first place? You enjoyed obeying Fuchs's orders. A lot. Don't deny it."

I can't. I suppose I could argue that it was Minerva who liked it, not me... but that's not the whole truth. Power is addictive, like any other drug. And too much of it can make you sick, like any other drug.

"I told you," I say quietly, looking at the table, "one day I just couldn't take it any longer. These friends, I knew them before Corvus. They'll help me get this information where it needs to go."

"And how are they going to do that?"

I don't answer. I just keep staring at the table.

He sighs, but it's not disappointment. More like he was expecting this. "And the CIA and the NSA? How are these friends going to protect you from them?"

I laugh, sharp and bitter. "They can't. No one can. But that's not the point."

The silence that follows is heavy. I can *feel* him breathing even though we're not touching. But he's so close the air he displaces rustles against me. I can't escape him when he's this close.

Finally he moves. His arm brushes mine, quick enough to shock me, then he's getting up, leaving me a path to flee.

"You can check your email tonight," he says in a rumbly tone. "I need to work now."

Without looking him in the eye, I slip out and dash up the stairs. With every fall of my feet on the steps, I pray that Deena answers today. This instant. And rescues me from this man.

CHAPTER 7

I told her I had to work, but that was a lie.

I can't concentrate, not with her so close. She's upstairs, quiet as a mouse, doing who knows what—and I'm just staring at my laptop screen, trying to go through these contracts while my brain listens as hard as it can for any noise from her.

It's getting close to dinnertime. I should call her down, tell her to check her email. Or offer her something to eat or drink. I didn't think to give her any breakfast or coffee this morning—Logan distracted me. And when lunch rolled around, I was too busy forcing myself to get any kind of work done to play the host.

She never came down, not to ask for anything. I'd suspect her of jumping overboard and swimming to freedom, but I didn't hear a splash. And I've still got her hard drive sitting on the table across from my laptop. I glance at it every so often, a reminder that she can't leave, not without that.

Logan's been texting me every hour, asking what I've done with her. My answer is always the same: nothing. I wonder if he's told the other Bastards that I have her here. I made him promise not to—all five of them on my back about this would drive me insane—but I'll have to tell them sooner or later. Minerva's wrecked or tried to wreck too many people they love to keep this a secret.

I want her to be gone before I tell them. *I had her, but she's gone.* Then there'd be nothing for them to do about it except yell at me for not telling them sooner. I can live with that.

I'm not sure I could live with them turning her in or taking that hard drive from her. I don't owe her anything… but when she was afraid and fleeing, she came to me. Thinking about it does strange things to my chest. Painful, uncomfortable things. I don't want to be responsible for her. I don't even like her.

I try one more time to read this contract that's due tomorrow, then finally give up. It should be fine since I've already been through it a few times. And with my eyes bouncing off the screen to look at anything but this contract every few seconds, I'm not going to catch any mistakes anyway. I close the window, then call up the web browser.

The home page starts to load automatically—the tech section of a major newspaper. There are several other sites that follow tech news more closely and in more depth, but I like to see what the laymen are saying about Silicon Valley too.

At Corvus, Dyne Steps out of the Shadows reads the first headline, which takes up the entire page. A headshot of Minerva is attached to the story, arms crossed, looking coolly professional.

My heart starts to pound. Has her escape leaked to the press? But what do they mean by *out of the shadows?*

I read it quickly, my eyes flying over the words. As I get to the end, my jaw tightens and my fists clench.

"Motherfucker," I mutter. I read through the story again, in case I've misunderstood any of it. But no, I haven't.

Minerva's fucking playing me. She's been lying since she got here. Which I should have fucking known.

"You want to explain this?" I yell up the stairs. "Grab your clothes when you come down, because you're out of here."

She comes down the stairs in her bare feet, wide-eyed and hair loose. A disguise, the better to pretend she's innocent. "What? What's going on?"

"Oh, just this press release from Corvus this very afternoon." The words burn as they leave my mouth. "They're very pleased and proud to announce the promotion of Minerva Dyne to COO. There's a great profile of you here too, where you tell the reporter how pleased you are to be taking on greater responsibility within the company."

She looks completely lost. "I don't understand. There was no promotion."

I shake my head because I'm so damn sick of her and her fucked-up boss getting me and the Bastards in the middle of their schemes. "Right. You disappear and Fuchs decides to promote you. That makes complete sense."

She flinches from my sarcasm like it's a physical blow. "I swear, I haven't been lying."

"No, but you haven't been telling the entire truth. Why would he do this if you've run away from him?" I smack my hand on the table when she doesn't respond. "Goddamn it, answer me!"

Her mouth opens, but nothing comes out. She looks... defeated. Rawly so. "He's trying to flush me out. I think." Her voice is low, uncertain. "Or not. I don't know what he's doing."

"You spent the past five years by his side, and you don't know what he's doing?"

Her skin is pale as milk. "I know he's angry. I definitely know that. And he's looking for me."

I close my eyes, try to pull back on my anger. This is all a trick, a show, something to fool and dazzle me while she and Fuchs pull off something. Only, I can't see what it would be and it fucking infuriates me. That and that I fell for her bull-shit, her damsel-in-distress act.

"He's not," I say. "Because he knows exactly where you are. He sent you here, didn't he? What was the hard drive about? What the hell are you two trying to pull?"

"I'm not—"

The pleading in her voice sickens me. "No. Shut up. Just stop. Go back to your master; tell him it won't work. And whatever you put on that laptop, it's not going anywhere. I'm dumping it into the canal once you're gone."

"No." She reaches for it. "Deena can't contact me if you do that."

Deena. I file that in the back of mind, a clue to investigate when I dissect this entire mess.

I grab the hard drive and shove it at her. "Take it. I don't need whatever bullshit you've put on it. And go."

I cross my arms, my jaw set. My pulse is ticking in my throat, my fingers, as anger flows through me. I was right to hate her all along. I let my guard down, thought she might actually be human under all that... and she wasn't.

The attraction I felt for her takes on a disgusting tint. Because even now I can't help but notice her, the trembling of her full lips, the tears collecting in her luminous eyes, the flutter of her pulse at the base of her neck.

"Fine." Some of her old defiance returns. "I'll leave. This was a mistake anyway."

As she slips her feet into her high heels, I have to bite back the urge to ask her where she'll go. Of course she's going back to Fuchs. Where else would she go?

But my idiot conscience keeps insisting *What if she doesn't? What if she's really on the run?*

My better sense tells it to shut up.

She walks to the door, her shoes clicking against the floor, her arms filled with her clothes and the hard drive.

She's still in my T-shirt and sweats. "I'll send the clothes back to you," she says with quiet dignity.

"Don't bother."

She swallows hard, her hand lingering on the doorknob. "Please don't tell anyone else I was here. And ask your brother to keep quiet too."

I shake my head. "You don't get to set terms."

She nods as if she was expecting that. And then she leaves without looking back or saying a word.

Once the door shuts behind her, my heart sinks. I know I did the right thing… but it still feels wrong.

CHAPTER 8

I'm way too exposed, but there's nothing I can do.

I can feel the cameras watching me as I walk down Third Street, their electronic eyes cold on the back of my neck. I keep my head down and stay in the areas where the cameras have blind spots.

It won't be enough though. The sun is out and the cameras can see everything. In a few hours, maybe even a few minutes, Fuchs will find me. He'll send his security detail to deal with me, and that will be that.

He won't kill me. He won't have to. He'll let his contacts in the government know what I stole, and I'll be very quietly and quickly convicted of espionage and sent to a supermax prison for years and years and years.

I just have to get this drive to someone before that happens. Maybe I should have left it with Elliot. He hates me, but once I end up disappeared, he'd know I was telling the truth. Which makes me sound like a little kid—*You'll be sorry once I'm dead!*

A T-line train comes rumbling past, only half full. It's going south, toward Mission Bay and Dogpatch and all the way toward Sunnydale. The train going north would be packed full of commuters, heading into the heart of the City.

I used to take the Muni all the time before Corvus. After Corvus, it was only Uber or company cars. Couldn't let yourself mingle with the commoners. Once I became Fuchs's assistant, I was too exalted for even the company buses that hauled people from their apartments in the City to the main Corvus building in South Bay and back again. There was a company car always at my disposal, along with a driver.

The urge to jump on the train, take it to the very end of the line, surges in me. I could watch the City go by and just breathe. Not think at all.

It's so tempting I actually turn toward the tracks without thinking. But the train is filled with cameras. It's the worst possible place for me to be.

Instead, I turn down Sixteenth Street, the medical school and hospital looming over me. Shuttles pull in and out of the traffic loop, and people rush from one building to another, all of them gripping coffee cups. No one seems to notice me even though I'm in sweatpants and a shirt that are way too big for me, a pile of clothes in my arms, and stiletto heels on my feet. Maybe they think I'm some new kind of hipster.

I keep close to the buildings, ducking under awnings and searching out the shadows. I can't completely hide from the cameras, but hopefully it will be enough to buy me some time.

My bigger problem is finding a place to go. I have some half-formed idea of showing up at Jay's place, or at least the last address I have for him, but God only knows if he'll be home. Or if he even still lives there. But his place is the closest and he was one of our original group, so I don't have much choice.

I'm leading Fuchs right to Jay if I do that, but maybe... maybe somehow Jay could hide the drive. Get it to someone else, someone who could release all the information I've gathered. It's a long shot, but it's all I've got.

The buildings of Mission Bay fall away, the 280 freeway

ramp rising overhead, blotting out the sun and filling the air with the thunder of cars. Under the freeway, the Caltrain tracks run north to the heart of the City, past the Third Street canal and Elliot's houseboat. There's nothing here but space for cars and trains. I take a moment to rest because there are no cameras, not in this no-man's-land. I see a homeless encampment several hundred feet away, in the empty space between the campus and the train tracks.

Nothing stirs anywhere though. It's eerily empty, one of the few places in San Francisco that is.

It's good, at least for me, but I can't help the shudder that comes over me. I don't want to be alone, not like this.

The arm of the train crossing lights up, the bell clanging angrily. Slowly the arm comes down, blocking me in on this side of the intersection.

Now I'm really freaked out. The Caltrain isn't like the Muni trains that run through the City—the Caltrain is pulled by massive, belching diesel engines that rattle your bones as they race by. The Caltrain is a serious goddamn train, one that kills plenty of people. At least once a month there's a story in the news about someone killed at a crossing.

I can't even see the train yet, but already the ground is trembling under my feet. I tuck myself against the massive concrete pillar holding up the freeway above me, wishing I could close my eyes.

Minerva wouldn't be frightened of the Caltrain. She'd sneer at anyone infantile enough to be frightened of a stupid train.

"Don't go on the tracks and you'll be fine," she'd say in a cold voice. "You're not dumb enough to go out there, are you?"

Except, I'm not Minerva. And I'm terrified.

I take short, jerky breaths through my nose, purse my lips to blow it all back out. I cannot have a panic attack here, so I won't. I simply won't.

The train appears around the bend, headlight bright and blinding. The stink of diesel fills my mouth, makes me want to gag.

It'll be past soon. You'll be just fine. I can't quite believe that though.

The rumble under my feet builds until my ribs are rattling with it. I grit my teeth, breathing through the gaps.

I'm going to be fine. I'm safe here by the pillar. Even if it feels like I'm going to shake apart.

And then something smashes into me from behind. My head snaps back, my arms flailing. My hips shove out past my knees, and I'm falling, nothing to stop me.

Panic claws through me as I reach for something to grab. My hand slips over the concrete of the pillar, finding nothing.

Oh God, I'm going to hit the ground. My heart is sick with the certainty. But at least—

A hand grabs my shirt, another the waistband of my pants. Thank God, someone's catching me.

The panic slows, adrenaline goes quiet. The hands lift me…

And I'm going over the rail crossing arm. Right onto the tracks.

I have just enough time to scream before I land. The gravel on the tracks tears into the skin of my palms, bites into my knees and hip. Fear is a high, sustained scream in me.

Move, move, movemovemove.

Behind me, the train blows its horn, warning me that it's coming to kill me. Out of the corner of my eye, I see a dark blur. A man or someone running away, elbows and legs pumping.

I don't have time to think about it. I don't even know if there's time to crawl off the track or if I should flatten myself in the middle and pray like hell.

Off the tracks. I'm taking my chances on that. I grab the rail, the metal cold and slick. I pull myself an inch forward, my feet scrabbling for purchase.

My knee hits something hard and square.

The hard drive.

I can't leave it. But if I take the time to look for it…

I reach between my legs, searching for that thing that cost me five goddamn years. My fingers find nothing but gravel, tiny pebbles lodging under my nails. I reach again.

The train's horn is now a constant blare. I hear a squeal, like metal on metal. The brakes—the train is actually trying to stop, although there's no time.

The side of my hand brushes against plastic. Thank fucking God.

I grab it. But it's too late. The train is too close.

Just as my hand closes around the drive, an arm snakes around my waist. I'm lifted, jerked really, up and off the tracks. And then my rescuer is running, dodging the crossing arm as he races to safety.

I can't breathe. From the panic, from the arm too tight around me. I choke and sputter, bile rising in my throat. I'm going to suffocate like this. I'd push the arm away, but I can't let go of the drive.

My vision starts to go gray. "Argh," I manage to get out, more a gargle than an actual noise.

The arm loosens, and I'm spun around. Hard hands clamp down on my shoulders.

"What the hell were you thinking?" Elliot's eyes burn with rage.

I open my mouth to answer, but then the gray goes to black and there's nothing.

The world comes back in a rush, on a full, deep breath. The air stings deep in my chest, in the back of my throat. But it's a good sting, a wonderful sting.

Pain means I'm still alive.

I'm alive and in Elliot's arms. I can see the underside of his jaw, tense and taut. His shirt is rough and warm against my cheek, and he's holding me as easily as if I were… something small and precious.

I blink away the last of the fog. We're on Owens Street, coming up to the roundabout where Owens turns into Channel Street. And from there Elliot's houseboat is only a minute or so away.

We're also terribly exposed. There's a camera on that streetlamp there, watching our every move.

"In the shadows," I croak. "They can see you out here."

Elliot says nothing, although his jaw cranks to a new level of *I'm really pissed.* He swerves toward the building, an ugly parking garage, which should hide us some.

"What the hell were you doing?" he asks after a few moments.

I tuck the drive closer to my chest. Somehow I've

managed to hold on to it. "I wasn't doing anything," I say. "Someone pushed me."

More than that—they *threw* me onto those tracks. My stomach flips just remembering.

"Not that," he growls. "I saw that."

The anger in his voice is low and rumbling, like it's coming up from somewhere deep, deep within him.

"How did you know where to find me?"

He misses a step but quickly recovers. "I was following you." Is that embarrassment there? Maybe? "I wanted to see where you'd go."

"You wanted to see if Fuchs would pick me up."

He shrugs and I bobble against his chest, his muscles dense and firm. "You can't blame me."

No, I suppose I can't. It still stings though.

"I wasn't going anywhere." *I have nowhere to go.* But it would be too pathetically clichéd to say that.

"I know," he says. "I was going to take you back home, when…" He goes hard as steel, all of him. "What the hell were you doing?"

"I told you—"

"The fucking hard drive." He jerks his chin at it like he wants to throw it into the street. "If you hadn't tried to grab it, you could have been off the tracks in time. It's not worth your life."

I laugh, because of course it is. What else were the past five years about except a sacrifice of myself? My life, the one I wanted to live?

"It's not funny. When I saw that asshole toss you over…"

I tilt my head to get a better look at him because— No, those aren't tears. He's just angry he had to interrupt his schedule of hating me to rescue me.

"Did you get a good look at him? Because he came up behind me. I didn't see anything."

Elliot shakes his head. "Once you were on the tracks, I could only look at you."

There's a long moment of quiet between us. He was probably only frightened or angry or panicking. It doesn't mean he cares or anything like that. He'd probably be more worried about a dog or something on the track than me.

But he still rescued me.

"Thank you," I say finally. "For saving me."

Elliot says nothing in return, but his throat bobs.

He gets me back to the houseboat so quickly I don't have time to worry about the cameras or someone else coming after us. He sets me down on the couch next to the windows lining the living room and then whips out his phone.

With a quick glance at me, he steps outside to make his call. I can hear the low murmur of his voice, intense, commanding. Whatever he's asking for, he wants it now.

I loosen my arms and take stock of the drive. That stupid, horrible hard drive that I almost died for. There's some dirt on it and some scuffs, but the case is intact. Hopefully nothing internal got damaged when I fell.

With shaking hands, I put the drive on the coffee table. I can't stop shivering suddenly as delayed shock rolls through me in a frigid wave. My teeth chatter as I wrap my arms around myself and clench my jaw to make it stop.

I was only out on the street a matter of minutes and he found me. More than found me—he tried to kill me.

Oh God. Oh God, oh God. I thought Fuchs would just send me to prison, but this...

Elliot comes back in, his gaze sharp and assessing when it lands on me. "A private security detail's coming. Five men, round the clock. And you're not stepping out of here, not until we..." He bites his lip. "Until I figure out the safest place for you." He looks out at the canal and then past it to the bridge and the bay. "Maybe I should have asked for a diver too. They have some ex-Navy SEALs on the team."

It's funny what he's done and the bit about the diver, but I'm also wound too tight to really laugh, so instead what comes out is more of a hiccup. "No, it's probably okay."

I have no idea if it is. I have no idea if anything is okay.

He gives me one last look, then goes upstairs to his bedroom. He comes back with a fluffy blanket that he wraps tightly around me, tucking me in as if I were a child.

When he's done, he stands up, looming over me. His mouth is stern, flat. "You almost died."

Another hiccup laugh. "I know. I was there." I can feel crazed laughter bubbling in my chest, trying to break out. Oh boy. After everything I've been through, a little murder attempt is what breaks me?

Elliot shakes his head. "No more smart remarks. No more arguing. I want the entire truth from you. Now."

"Or what, you'll throw me out again?"

He leans in so close I can smell mint on his breath. And a hint of something warmer. "That was your only warning. No. Smart. Remarks." He gives me just enough space to breathe. "And no, you're not going anywhere."

That's the biggest threat he's ever made to me. It's exactly what I asked for, but not like this.

"Fine." I stand up, toss away the blanket. My shoes are gone, probably lost in the street somewhere, so he's got at least a foot on me. I don't care. "Let me tell you everything. You want a confession?"

He doesn't reply, just keeps that stony stare.

I'm on a roll though. I tap my chest, hard. "Here, then, this is what you wanted. I've turned people out of their homes, old people, poor people, because Fuchs wanted a building torn down. It blocked his office view, see, and he didn't like it. They begged me—one woman even had an oxygen tank— but I smiled in all their faces and signed the eviction notices. And down that building came. Nothing else was put there."

He says nothing.

"Gordian Development didn't come to us—we went to them. Oh, have we got the scheme for you! I told them. All that riffraff, the people who can't afford to live here anymore, those living reminders of how you drove out anyone who wasn't rich—I can get rid of them for you. Make those property values soar."

He still says nothing.

"They wanted more money of course, but what they really wanted was their guilt washed away. All those people they'd pushed out into the streets—they didn't want to see them anymore, didn't want the reminder of what they'd done. And I gave them that. Without hesitation."

Finally he moves. Just a twitch of his mouth.

"Oh, there's so much more," I promise. "Do you know how many suicides we have a month at Corvus? It's a lot. And when someone can't take it anymore—the long hours, the lack of freedom, the secrecy—and walks up the stairs to the roof, I'm the one who goes to the family. I give them their blood money, so little as to be an insult, and I make it very, very clear that if they sue Corvus for anything, I'll bury them. Personally."

Those were the worst. I thought I hid my old self so deeply in Minerva she'd never come out again, but seeing those families… threatening them like that…

I suppose it proved I was still human after all. Just not human enough to stop doing it.

Elliot is shaking his head. "That's not what I meant."

"Liar." I snap that out like the tail of a whip. "That's exactly what you want. To hear all the ways you should hate me. It feels so good to hate me, doesn't it?"

"Stop." His voice is deeper than I've ever heard. Deep enough to vibrate all the way to my toes.

"No." What's he going to do about my smart remarks, kick me out? Besides, I almost died by Caltrain a few minutes ago. Something in me went sideways when that happened. I'm not Minerva, and I'm not who I used to be.

I'm someone else entirely, and she wants to keep going.

"I'm not done." I ball my hands into fists. "I'm not anywhere near finished."

"Shut. Up." His expression is stark, his skin blanched.

"Why don't you make me?"

The dare I throw out bounces between us, springing off him, then me, then him again. Everything shifts, like the boat has tilted.

He's breathing too hard. We haven't even done anything —he shouldn't be breathing like that. "Stop talking."

It's not a threat, more like a long-awaited promise.

"I'm not going to shut up." Another promise.

He breathes heavily, too hard to be a pant. His eyes are dark pools, his face so close to mine. His control is just barely there. "Stop."

"No. You'll have to shut me up if you want me to stop." I shouldn't taunt him, not when he's so clearly on edge, but I can't help myself. "You'll have to cover my mouth, shove something in it."

Another heavy, serrated breath, more animal than human. "I warned you."

I snort. "What are you going to do? I know what you want to do." The image blooms in my mind before I can halt it. "You want to shut me up with your cock. Your hard, thick cock in my mouth, finally making me quiet. Under your control."

Minerva would never say that. The girl I used to be wouldn't either.

But when I say it, I mean every word.

Elliot grabs me by the neck, his hand so big, so heavy. I tilt my face up, offering my mouth to him. He wants to take me, and I want to be taken.

CHAPTER 10

This woman is all fire.

I told myself when I first encountered her that she was cold to her very bones and that was why I had such a reaction to her. That my reaction was all repulsion.

But I lied. My reaction was more than that, just as I sensed Minerva was more than a cold, unfeeling automaton.

She provokes me, and she always has. But now I have her.

Her lips move against mine, soft, full. The rest of her is slim, almost angular, but those lips…

Her taunts hit too close to home. Because, yeah, I jerked it to dreams of those lips wrapped around my cock, her mouth hot and wet on my skin.

She's kissing me like she had some dreams of her own. Of my tongue in her mouth—just like it is now—my hands sliding up her torso, cupping her breasts—like they are now —and her pussy, tight and achy. Needing my fingers.

My hand tightens in her hair, pulling her close with a greedy urgency I hardly recognize in myself. I'm a careful, considerate lover. I don't maul my partners.

But goddamn, I want to consume this woman. It's like she reaches inside me and snaps my reserve right in half.

A little moan escapes her, half pain, half pleasure. I tug her hair again, hard enough to let her know I'm not letting go, and her mouth opens, giving me full access.

Her shirt—*my* shirt—slips off one shoulder, revealing inches of gorgeous skin. I bend over, run my tongue over the arches of her collarbones. She shivers, and I smile with triumph.

One tug from me and that shirt could be on the floor. Her breasts are hard against my chest, her nipples tight points driving me mad, and I can tell she's not wearing a bra. Another tug and the sweatpants could join the shirt. And she'd be entirely bare to me.

She couldn't hide then. I'd see all of her.

The thought beats in my blood, making my cock stiffen. She licks into my mouth, bold as anything, and I growl. Actually growl, like some kind of rutting animal.

"Yes," she whispers. "Do that again."

Fuuuck. The way she says that, all thready and broken… I bend her over my arm, arch that body of hers into mine, just like I imagined.

There's a sharp rap at the door, then another. Not someone coming to visit but here on official business then.

Her eyes go wide, shock flooding her expression. She wriggles her hands between us, levering me away.

I let her go just enough to make sure she won't fall, then call out, "Yes?"

"Just wanted to let you know we're in place, sir" comes from the other side of the door.

The security detail is here. Something unknots in my gut. If Fuchs or his goons were to come through that door, I'd fight like hell to keep them from Minerva, but it's good to have backup.

Minerva looks up at me, licks her lips. The desire is gone, replaced by reality. And a sad fearfulness.

I lower both of us to the couch, keeping her in my arms. Somehow I know she needs the comfort. Even if it comes from me.

"It will all be fine now," I promise. "No one will get through those guys."

She leans against me, breathing in time with my inhales and exhales. Somehow, in only a day or so, we've fallen into the same rhythm. "I'm afraid." She confesses it like it's something to be ashamed of.

"You weren't before?" Because she had been, soaking wet and running to me in the middle of a storm. Even when I tried my hardest to keep hating her, that fear tore at me.

"I was, but… not like this. I thought he'd only send me to prison."

"He can do that?"

She sends me a look that says *Oh, you sweet summer child.* "You read those documents, saw who he controls in the government. He can do anything to me through them."

"It wouldn't be legal." God, it's such a stupid thing to say, but I can't help it. Even after everything I've seen, I still cling to some faith in the law. *We don't disappear people. We don't extrajudicially murder citizens. We're better than that.*

I know they're all lies, but some part of me wishes they weren't.

She laughs, her eyes closed. "Fuchs is beyond the legal system."

"Tell me—" I stop, gentle what I was about to say. I can't command this woman, not anymore. "Can you tell me more about what happened? At Corvus?"

"I didn't tell you the worst thing I did."

Jesus. I swallow down my reaction. "I don't mean that. I know there's more you haven't told me. I meant about you, your friends. Tell me what you can. What you trust me with."

I can't say that I trust her, and I'm certain she doesn't

trust me, not really, but we've got to start somewhere. That hard drive sitting on the table is like a ticking time bomb, and somehow we've got to defuse it. Or else she's going to end up dead.

My breath hitches. Goddamn, but she was so close today. I'm going to have nightmares for the rest of my life about that train.

Her hand slips up my chest, then hooks around my neck. As if she's anchoring herself. Then she pushes me away. Sits up, alone on the couch, putting a foot of space between us.

It's the right thing to do—I was practically cuddling her, which I don't do, not ever, and we're not... not even friends. I cross my arms, putting even more distance between us.

"This was the plan all along." Her voice is stronger, steadier. "For me to work at Corvus for a while, gather and smuggle out as much internal information as I could, and then we'd expose it. As a way to stop them. We knew even then that they were up to some bad shit."

"A while? How long was that supposed to be?" Five years is a very long time for a plan like this.

She shrugs. "A year. At most. But the higher up the ladder I moved, the more awful shit I found. I hoarded it like a treasure. And at the end of each year I thought, 'Just a little longer. A little more evidence. And then I'll be done.'"

"What did your friends say?" And who the fuck lets a woman like this—their friend, for Christ's sake—work for a monster like Fuchs for so long?

"Nothing." She raises a clear gaze to mine. "I had no contact with them the entire time. It was too risky."

My mouth drops open. If that's true...

I fight the impulse to disbelieve her. If this is all a story— and it could be—she's gone to some lengths to make me believe. But on some level, it's too fantastical. No one has the resolve to do what she said she did.

But if it *is* true, she's been completely alone the past five years.

"You have no idea if your friends are still… in on it?"

She shakes her head. "That's why I need to contact them. But carefully. I don't want to lead Fuchs to them."

I frown. "But… he'll find them anyway. Everybody's connected online these days."

"He won't."

She says it with such certainty. And it hits me—her real name is not Minerva. She's been living an utterly consuming lie—as an entirely different person—for five years.

And she isn't going to tell me about it.

I lean back, resettle my arms. I'm not going to let on that I've figured her out. I'm definitely not going to ask what her real name is. No, letting Finn do some digging in the dark corners of the internet will be much more effective. But I will get her true identity somehow.

"How many were in on this?"

"There were four of us, including me."

So she's only got three people in this entire world who might help her. Emphasis on the might.

"And your family? Didn't they notice when you disappeared?"

"We've had no contact since—for a while." There's not a flicker of anything on her face. It looks like the family got left behind a long time ago if it doesn't hurt anymore.

Although, my dad's been dead for years, and I'm still fucked up about it. So time isn't the best measure.

"Can you contact the others?" Five years is a long time. Emails change, phones get disconnected, people move. And her friends might not be committed to the cause any longer. Especially with the jail time they might be looking at, not to mention the legal fees. Whistle-blowing isn't easy.

"I have some emails I could try."

I grab my laptop, hand it to her. "Send them messages. All

of them. I assume you already know what security measures to use."

She nods, then gets to it. Her hair is down, all around her shoulders, and she hasn't hiked the shirt back up. At some point she crossed her legs, the better to balance the laptop.

I can't say she looks younger or more relaxed. Just different. Someone else entirely than Minerva.

"You can't tell anyone about this." She doesn't look up from the computer screen.

"Pardon?"

"The other Bastards." When she meets my gaze, the old Minerva is back. "I know you're planning to, but you can't."

"This thing has spun way out of your control. And mine. You can't set any rules." Let her think I'm the world's biggest asshole, but that's not a condition I'm going to meet. I need help with this. And so does she, beyond those shitty friends of hers.

Her jaw tightens, but she doesn't argue. I'm under no illusions—she's not agreeing with me. She's saving the fight for later.

"Done." She closes the laptop and takes a deep breath. "Hopefully they'll answer."

"How did you find these people?" I don't know anything about them besides that they put her up to this.

"We're young and idealistic." She smiles sadly. "At least we were. And like attracts like. I'm sure you have a big circle of stuffy lawyer types you hang out with."

I don't. My work keeps me too busy. And once the day is done, I only want to come home to this quiet island that's all mine.

Before I can answer, she yawns. Before she covers her mouth, I see the flash of her teeth, the pink of her tongue.

"You need to rest." I gesture to the stairs, sharper than I mean to. But the sight of her tongue does things to me, things I can't indulge. "You've been through a lot, and you're probably in shock."

If I dared, I'd call a doctor in to look at her. But it's too risky. Fuchs knows she's here now, and he might try something.

She stares down at her palms. "Yeah. And clean up my cuts."

Shit. I fucking forgot about that. Yeah, I am the world's biggest asshole.

"I'll do it."

Before she can protest, I'm up the stairs, rummaging through the medicine cabinet. When she comes in behind me, the hairs on my neck stand up. Along with other parts of me.

I hand over the bandages and antiseptic. "Come out when you're done," I say gruffly.

While she's in the bathroom, I pull down the sheets. She needs rest and lots of it. When she comes out, I don't look directly at her. "Get some sleep. We'll talk more later. And remember, the security guards are right outside. No one's getting in here."

Without a word, she climbs into the bed. The soles of her feet wink at me as she does, small, pale, bare.

"Thank you." It's the first thing she's said since she came up the stairs.

"Just get some sleep." I duck my head, turn toward the stairs.

She grabs my wrist. "Could you… could you stay here? Just until I'm asleep?" Her tongue darts out to wet her lips. Her expression is nakedly vulnerable. Pleading, like she's expecting me to refuse.

I clear my throat. "Sure."

Her hand releases, but I can still feel the imprint of her fingers. I settle into the chair by the bed, the one that I like to read in at night. There's a book sitting on the nightstand, a thriller I've been working through. I could pick it up, get some reading done while I wait.

Instead, I watch her as she settles in, pulling the blankets over her head, turning to one side, then the other. She sighs, the sound thick with weariness.

And then she's quiet and still.

CHAPTER 11

I'm so tired, but there's a light stabbing behind my eyelids.

I frown and roll over. My heart kicks when my hand connects with something. Something warm, rough with hair.

A hand.

My eyes snap open. Next to me on the bed, lying on top of the covers, is Elliot. He's still in his clothes, one arm tossed over his head, and he's… he's asleep.

I shouldn't be shocked. Everyone sleeps, even Elliot. I know he did it on the couch downstairs just last night.

But tonight he's in this bed. With me.

I bite my lip, remembering so pathetically asking him to stay. But my hands were hurting and so was my knee, and the panic had settled like a hard rock in my stomach. I knew the security guards were outside, keeping watch, but I needed someone closer. I needed him.

When I closed my eyes, he was in the chair. I could tell he sat in it a lot because he settled right into place, like the chair had curved to fit him. And with him watching over me, I slept.

My dreams were terrible. I kept falling from great heights, never hitting the ground. Just falling, over and over again, forever. My stomach feels like it really happened, like it will never get right side up again.

I sit up, the covers pulling where Elliot is pinning them down. He's sleeping on his stomach, one leg hiked up, his arm crooked over his head. He looks like he fell asleep before he even hit the bed.

Maybe he did. Maybe he was so tired he blindly went for the bed, forgetting that I was here. He didn't even have the energy to pull back the covers. I wonder how often he does this, sleep on top of the bed fully clothed. I would have guessed never if I weren't seeing it with my own eyes.

He's got an alarm clock by the bed, the time picked out in neon-red light. I bet he's one of those people who practices digital hygiene and never brings his phone into his bedroom. So no alarm clock on the phone then, just the old-fashioned one.

The time is 3:28 a.m. Way too early to get up. Way too late to be getting to bed.

The light that was stabbing me is a table lamp. Next to it is a book, marker peeping out from about halfway through. He must have been reading while he kept me company. Then, probably falling asleep in his chair, he collapsed into the bed.

I've had a terrible, awful day, but his hasn't really been any better. He didn't want me on his doorstep any more than I wanted to be there. And then he had to keep me from being murdered.

My eyes narrow as I realize Elliot never called the cops. Instead, he had some mercenaries come in at the snap of his fingers. And yeah, they have to be mercenaries. Ex-Navy SEALs don't just work for any old security firm.

Maybe he does believe me about Fuchs being able to reach into almost anywhere to find me.

He shifts, his eyelids fluttering. Something halfway between a breath and a noise comes from him.

I reach over and switch off the lamp. It's kind of nice,

having everything within arm's reach. It should feel crowded, but it really doesn't. I can see why a houseboat would appeal to him.

But when everything goes pitch-black, my heart shimmies up my throat. I know there's nothing out there waiting to grab me, crawling up the stairs on hands and knees to stalk me, but my stupid panic response won't believe it.

I can't help it—I whimper before I can stop myself.

Elliot stirs next to me. "Is fine," he slurs, still half-asleep. "I didn't go anywhere."

His big hand reaches out, catches my shoulder. His grip is clumsy but reassuring. With a gentle push, he brings me back down to the bed. I don't resist.

"Sleep." It's a command, even though it sounds like his eyes are still closed.

I fold my hands over my belly and stare into the dark. I'm not ready to sleep, not by a long shot, but the panic is leaking away.

He wants me to tell him everything. The entire plan, my friends' names, even my own real name. I could do it too. Just dump everything in his lap, including the hard drive, take off for some nonextradition country, and let the Bastards deal with all of it.

But I won't. That hard drive is mine, the burden entirely on my shoulders. I'm not giving it up. Or, more accurately, I can't.

I close my eyes, but instead of darkness, there's a train light bearing down on me, too fast to escape. Every muscle in my body goes tight with the impulse to flee. But I can't. I can't escape my own head.

Breathe. Just breathe. If I can keep pulling oxygen in, I can get through this. Inhale, exhale.

But the train keeps coming.

There's a snuffling noise next to me as the entire bed

shifts. Elliot tosses an arm over me, landing across my waist in the exact spot where he grabbed me on the tracks.

"Sleep." It's the same growl he used when he was kissing me. Oh, that growl. It does magical things to every inch of me.

I shouldn't have said that to him, that thing about his cock in my mouth. I could blame the shock, but… but I kind of meant it. And when he kissed me, I knew he'd been thinking the exact same thing.

I didn't tell him the worst thing I did as Minerva. I never got the chance.

Okay, I need to stop this. My thoughts are bouncing through my skull I'm so keyed up. Focus is what I need. Focus on my breathing.

But instead, my mind keeps slipping back to the kiss. And I'm too tired to stop it. At least it's not the train.

So I fall asleep remembering how hot, how hungry Elliot's mouth was on mine, his hands claiming my body while his arm anchors me to his bed.

CHAPTER 12

I'm terrified to leave her, but in the end I have no choice.

It's Monday and I can't miss the morning partners' meeting at Bastard Capital. I have to tell them what's happened, get their ideas on how to help Minerva. And what to do with the hard drive.

First though, I have to tell Minerva what I'm about to do.

When she comes down the stairs, I'm already dressed, ready to head in. Suit, tie, briefcase, a coffee in my hand. My armor all in place.

She pauses on the middle step, a shy smile frozen on her face. "I'm sorry I fell asleep so early." Pink stains her cheeks. "I didn't mean to take your bed."

"It's fine," I say, way too gruffly. "I, uh, should have moved to the couch. Sorry."

I also shouldn't have *held* her while I slept, but I was exhausted. Out of my mind with sleep deprivation. And she was close and soft.

And yes, I'm wildly attracted to her.

"It's okay." She's staring at her feet. "I was having some crazy dreams. It helped."

That sensation in my chest might be my heart melting.

I freeze it cold again by reminding myself that she's spent the past five years successfully lying to the most paranoid man in the world. She could be faking all this, because she's a goddamn professional at it. Olympic level.

I need to get all this out of my head and laid out in front of the Bastards before I can reassemble it into something that makes sense. I also need to figure out this whole CIA/NSA wrinkle. And the murder-attempt thing too.

And kissing her and sleeping in the same bed with her. But that I'll have to puzzle through on my own.

I lift the briefcase in my hand. "I have to go into the office. I have to take my laptop, but there's uh…" I spin around, looking for something for her to do. There's no TV, no extra computer—not that I'd let her on the internet without supervision—and not really any other entertainment.

"I'll be fine," she says quickly.

"There are books in the cabinets above the bed." Thank God I remembered those.

Her mouth twists. "More thrillers?"

So she saw the book on the nightstand. "You don't like them?"

"No, they're fine. I haven't been able to read much lately." A tiny frown wrinkles her brow. "A day spent reading should be fun." But she sounds very uncertain about the prospect.

I have to admit, I'd go stir crazy being stuck inside without any work to occupy me and only some books. "I'll be back as soon as I can."

"Can I check my emails before you go?"

"Yeah." I take out the laptop and slide it across the kitchen counter to her. I can tell by her expression as she stares at the screen that it's not good news.

"Nothing." Her lips tremble as she shuts the laptop. "But I still have two days, right?"

It's a joke, but I don't find it funny. And I don't think she does either. "There's no more time limit." I take a deep inhale, my gaze cutting to the hard drive sitting on the coffee table. "I have to take the drive with me."

I figured I should just come out and say it rather than dancing around it, but I didn't count on Minerva's reaction. Her eyes go wide, her cheeks go white, and for a second I think she might faint.

"It's not yours." But it's clear in her tone that she knows she can't stop me.

"You can't do this on your own. After yesterday, you have to realize that." I motion to the laptop. "And your friends aren't going to come through."

"You don't know that." The old defiance is back.

"My friends are some of the most powerful people in tech." I put the laptop back in my briefcase. "And they hate your boss. So aren't they the exact people who should be looking at that drive?"

"He's not my boss."

"Right. Does he know that yet? Because you just got a big promotion. Yesterday."

She stares at me for a long moment. "I really don't like you."

I smile as I take the drive and shove it into my briefcase. "The feeling is mutual."

For half a moment she seems to smile. And I realize I'm kind of smiling too. A real smile, not the edged one I gave her a second ago. We're just… mutually *disliking* each other here.

Right. Whatever this is, I need to get to work. I brush past her as I walk to the door. Confusion grabs me for a moment. How should I say goodbye? Just wave and go?

Give her a kiss? My body really loves that idea.

"Don't leave. For any reason." I point at her as I say it.

"I won't." She gives my briefcase a longing look. "I can't

take the drive back, but I can ask… Don't let anything happen to it. Please."

"I'm going to make a copy of it. A secure copy," I add at her expression. Actually, I won't be doing it; I'll leave that to Finn since I'm not a computer guy. "And we'll start researching your… legal options."

Her lips are so thin they're going white, and she's staring at her clenched hands. "I can't stop you from doing any of that."

The softness of her voice, the way she's standing, is all calculated to play on my sympathies. I know that, but my conscience still snaps like a rubber band. Which pisses me off.

"No, you can't." I wrench open the door. "Don't even think of trying to get past these guys outside."

She wants to pretend to be a wounded prisoner? Fine, we'll play that game.

As I walk out, I keep one ear cocked for a snappy comeback from her. I'm almost disappointed when I don't get one.

Two hours later, I'm sitting in my usual spot at the conference table at Bastard Capital, one slice of organic honeydew melon on a plate at my right, a cup of the special roast we—and only we—get at my left. My pens are lined up exactly parallel to each other, and there's a fresh legal pad in front of me. I'm in my element, the place I'm in control, where everything fits as it should.

My house used to be a place where I'm in control, but now that it's been invaded…

Minerva's invaded here too though, without even being present. Because every single one of the Bastards—even unflappable Anjie, and Paul on the videoconference screen— are staring at me, wide-eyed and openmouthed. Completely speechless.

Logan is less shocked though. More like grimly satisfied,

as if to say *See? You should have kicked her out.* He doesn't know about the murder attempt yet. Maybe that will change his mind. Maybe not.

"She's in your house?" Mark is the first to recover.

"Under armed guard," I say.

Logan barks out a laugh. "So you finally came to your senses."

I glare at him. "Someone tried to kill her."

"You, right?" That's Paul, calling in via video chat from Taipei. "You tried to put a stake in her heart. Because that's the only way to deal with her."

This is not going how I'd planned. "Can everyone shut up and let me finish?"

"No." Finn crosses his beefy arms. "This is fucking Minerva Dyne we're talking about. And you're just like, 'Oh, she's at my place, no biggie.' Did she hypnotize you or something?"

I clench my fist, remembering that train bearing down on her. Okay, I know she's not innocent, not by a long shot, but she didn't fake that.

Anjie clears her throat. "We should let him talk."

There's some grumbling, but everyone shuts their mouth. Such is the magic of Anjie—she can control six raging assholes and their billionaire egos.

"She came to my place two nights ago. Alone, while it was pouring rain. She'd walked there."

"She didn't melt when the water hit her?" Logan mutters.

Since it's under his breath, I ignore that. "She was clearly afraid and desperate. She said she was the mole."

Finn snorts. But Paul's eyes go wide, like he's just realized something.

"And she had this." I pull out the hard drive, plunk it on the table. "It's everything she took from Corvus. All the things they don't want anyone to see."

Finn puts his hands flat on the table and stands up. He's practically vibrating with the urge to crack that thing open.

"Have you looked through it?" Dev asked. He's back to calm, impenetrable Dev.

I nod. "There's some explosive stuff on there. Like a turf war between the CIA and the NSA over Corvus's domestic spying program."

"Fuck," Mark huffs out.

"Exactly."

"Why you?" Dev's tone is sharp. "Why did she come to you with this?"

"She said it was the last place Fuchs would look. But he knows she's there now."

"How?" Dev's frowning.

I shift in my chair. What happened isn't my fault, and she would have died if I hadn't been there, but I still feel guilty. "You all saw the Corvus COD announcement?"

They all nod. Of course they did.

"What's up with that?" Logan asks.

"I don't know. But... I threw her out when I saw it. I figured it was all some elaborate scheme by her and Fuchs, although I couldn't see what the goal was. I... I followed her to see if Fuchs or someone else from Corvus would pick her up. Then I'd know." I stare at my hands. "No one did. She just walked through the streets, like she had nowhere to go. And when she got to the Caltrain crossing, the one at 16th... Someone pushed her—no, threw her—onto the tracks. I only just pulled her off in time."

There's a long beat of silence. "Fuck," Mark says again, longer and lower.

"Yeah." I flex my fingers. "It was intense. I couldn't get a good look at the guy who did it, and I couldn't go after him. But I took her home and called in the security detail."

"You could have called us," Logan says, anger in his voice. "Jesus, I had no idea."

"I handled it."

"We know you can," Finn says, "but we're here for you, dude. Can I get into that drive now?"

I shove it toward him. "Go ahead. Can you make a secure copy too? Minerva's worried about it."

Finn looks like a kid seeing a dirt bike with his name on it under the Christmas tree. "She really sent Doc all that stuff about the panopticon and the back door into Corvus?"

"She claims she did."

"Maybe she's not all bad then."

I've already started to suspect that myself.

"What was she planning to do with this information?" Dev asks. There's something in his tone I don't like, but I can't pin it down.

"She had some people she was working with. Before Corvus. I think she's planning to release all this information with their help. But she has to get in touch with them first."

"She's been at Corvus for at least five years," Mark says. "And she's been working on this the entire time?"

"That's what she told me." I'd been planning to tell them before this, but now that I'm about to, I'm suddenly unsure. "And Minerva's not her real name. She didn't tell me that, but I'm pretty sure it's not."

It's out and it's too late to pull it back, but I feel like I've betrayed her in some way. Which is ridiculous. She's the one who's not telling the truth, at least not the entire truth.

"I'll get on that too," Finn says.

He'll probably find her real identity. Finn's got resources in the dark web that I don't even want to know about.

"She can't be allowed to release this information," Dev says. "Don't give her that drive back."

I start to protest how I can't just take it from her when I realize that's exactly what I've done. Everything Dev and the rest of them are suggesting is what I thought about doing in the first place… But somehow without Minerva here to fight back, it feels like they're ganging up on her. And I'm the only one left to defend her.

Which she doesn't need. Not at all.

"Why can't the information be released?" I haven't decided if I'll give the drive back, but I'm not letting Dev make that decision unilaterally.

No one answers because they're all too busy agreeing with Dev and asking Finn to look for this or that on the drive.

I'm used to being the odd one out here—the only lawyer among the programmers, a guy who can barely code a website. But I'm also the only one here who really understands the legal implications of what Minerva's done. And just how much judicial firepower is going to be trained on her.

"We'll get you a hotel room," Logan is saying to me. "And leave her there, on your boat, with the guards. I know you don't like hotels, but it'll be temporary."

"I've got an apartment he can use," Paul says over the line.

Mark nods. "Yeah, keep her nice and secure. And then we can figure out who'll take her."

"Take her where?" I ask.

"I wonder who she was going to sell this to," Finn says, holding up the drive to stare at it.

"You don't believe the whistle-blower story?" Dev asks.

"Her? Naw. Minerva is only ever looking out for Minerva."

I set my hands palm down on the table. "She. Was. Almost. *Murdered.*"

The room gets very quiet.

"We know," Logan says, but I don't think he gets it. "Still, you don't have to stay there with her. She's fine and safe with the guards."

"Right." Finn sets the drive down. "You can get your own

space, and in the meantime, she's secure while we figure out… something."

It makes perfect sense. I don't want to be that close to her even though I kissed her, and she doesn't want to be that close to me. I was the choice of last resort.

"She needs clothes," I blurt out.

"I'll arrange to send over everything she'll need. And someone to check on her," Anjie says.

I notice that Anjie isn't going herself. Minerva is going to be… *sealed up* in my house, with no contact with the outside world. They're going to make my home into a prison cell.

"I'm not leaving."

Again, there's silence. They're readjusting, fitting their plans to me and my declaration.

"We could move her," Mark says slowly. "But it's—"

"We're not moving her and I'm not leaving." Everything snaps back into place as I take control of the situation. "There's space for both of us. And she… she tells me things."

I almost said she trusted me, but that's not true.

Dev sits back. "You think she'll tell you more about this plan of hers?"

"Possibly. I've certainly gotten more out of her than any of the rest of you." I might not be able to crack all the secrets of that hard drive, but I can get at some of hers.

Logan snickers. "As if you'd want any more of *her.*"

I see red. That's the only way to describe it. Logan's made me this mad before, but like, when I was five and he took my Legos.

I grab hold of my anger, shove it away. "Anjie, could you bring the clothes yourself?" My voice is steadily neutral. "She's…" I try to think of how to describe her size. Smaller, more vulnerable than you might guess. But that's not a size. "She's shorter than January. Thinner than Callie. And can you bring some bathroom stuff?"

"Toiletries? Yeah, I can do that. And I can find some clothes that will work."

I nod, then rise from my chair. "I need that drive back when you're done. I'm going to start researching Minerva's options."

No one stops me as I leave. But I don't make the mistake of assuming that they've given up on their original plans.

I'm going to have to talk to Elliot about his internet security. But I'll have to do it after I leave here since his lapses are my opportunities.

Once he left, I went in search of the books he mentioned. I wasn't going to try my chances at getting past the guards, so I figured I should find something to do.

And I did. Behind the stacks of books, I found an old e-reader, clearly unused. I bet he got it as a gift, turned it on just to be polite, then tossed it aside in favor of paper books.

I plugged it in and switched it on and then did a dance when it immediately connected to the Wi-Fi.

So here I am on the internet when I'm not supposed to be. The operating system on this thing isn't exactly sophisticated, so I can't do too much—and the little keyboard is absolutely torturous—but I have managed to check the fake email accounts I set up. No reply from anyone.

I don't let myself be disappointed by that.

Next, I read every news article I can find on my "promotion." My position at Corvus wasn't a normal one. I wasn't an engineer or developer or even a vice president—there was no official title attached to me. According to HR, I was classified as a specialist, but my specialty was Arne Fuchs and him alone. I did what he wanted, made his wishes happen. People might have been even more afraid of me than they were of him.

Promotions weren't a thing that happened to me. Sometimes I got a raise, which I only found out about when I got my paychecks. Otherwise, Fuchs gave me orders and I gave him results. There were no performance reviews.

So giving me the title of COO is a tactic of his. He's trying to make me do something. Probably come back. Or be dumb enough to expose myself so he can catch me.

But he knows I'm not that stupid. And he knows exactly what I took, what's at risk for me here. Perhaps he's so angry he's flailing. It's not something he does often—too much of the world bends itself to his whims—but it does happen.

Unless…

I drum my fingers on the dining table. Outside I can see two large men, earpieces in, strolling in front of the houseboat. Occasionally one of them hops onto the deck, looks around.

I wonder what the neighbors think of this. Because these guys aren't trying to be discreet.

That's Elliot's problem though, not mine.

And I think I know now why Fuchs did it. It wasn't to flush me out—it was to cast suspicion on me. He might have guessed that I went for help when I left. And that whomever I contacted might not be so eager to believe me.

If that was the plan, it worked. Elliot tossed me out without a second thought. Then Fuchs struck.

I'm beginning to believe that I'm not getting out of this intact. It's either prison or death at the end of this road. I suppose that's karma coming for me after everything I've done. *I didn't mean the bad things; it was all to stop more bad things*—justice won't care about my excuses.

Time to google my friends, see if I can find anything about them.

Deena doesn't seem to be anywhere on social media. There're a few profiles with the same name, but they're not her. And there's nothing about a job anywhere or former addresses or any of it. She must be periodically wiping her internet presence. There's nothing there that will help me contact her, but if she's being so cautious, she must still be committed to our cause.

Next I look up Chad. Instantly I get a bunch of social media profiles—and they're definitely his. Pictures of his wife and kid are prominent on them. His son is a toddler and amazingly cute. So he married and started a family.

It's not what I would have expected, given how Chad used to talk about relationships and monogamy. I guess he found someone to change his mind.

His Facebook profile says he works at some place called Starline Enterprises. That website says they're a company that specializes in "corporate solutions." I have no idea what those might be. I can't imagine Chad, at least the Chad I knew, enjoying a job like that. But the Chad I knew seems to be gone.

Even if Chad contacts me, I can't message him back. With a family, he can't get pulled into this.

Finally I search for Reagan. The first thing that comes up is a GoFundMe page. And the update is bad.

Reagan is dead. She got sick—cancer. Couldn't afford the treatment, so she started a fund-raising page. But… but she couldn't quite raise enough.

So she died.

I have to put the e-reader down so I can breathe. Reagan was one of my best friends. It hurt like hell to cut her off when I went to Corvus. I didn't contact her first because she had enough on her plate—lots of family issues.

I used to go to their house for Thanksgiving. Her family was loud, prone to fights, but Reagan used to roll her eyes and laugh about it. After being on my own for so many holidays, I loved it even as it overwhelmed me. But if Reagan hadn't been there, it wouldn't have been half as fun.

And she's gone. I didn't get to say goodbye. Because I was still selfishly absorbed in my mission.

Once more, I summon Minerva and push the pain of losing my friend aside. There's no time to mourn. I have to finish this. I can't get emotional. I don't have to keep pretending to be Minerva, but I still need some of her tools.

Perhaps it's time to cut all my old ties. To keep going like I have been: completely alone.

I call up Twitter and start scrolling through several journalists' feeds. More than one has their secure messaging information in their profile. Once I get the drive back, I could send one of them everything.

I'll be caught even if it's sent anonymously. Fuchs will make sure of that. And his friends at the CIA and the NSA will be furious that I spoiled their scheme. People like that don't let grudges go.

But at least when I go down, I'll only take myself.

Of course, that's assuming the journalists would even print the story. And that the watchdogs in government who are supposed to stop these kinds of things do.

I get up, start to pace. The sweatpants slide down my hips, and I just catch them in time. Having proper clothes that fit would be nice. My suit was completely ruined by the rain, which I'm strangely grateful for. Putting on Minerva's clothes again isn't something I want to do.

I want new clothes. I want to leave the shell of Minerva behind finally.

In prison, I'll get some nice orange jumpsuits. I laugh to myself about that. Be careful what you wish for.

I flick through Twitter more, looking for the activists I used to know. Some are gone, probably banned, and some haven't posted in years. A few are still there though, still posting about the things in the dark that the government and corporations don't want you to know about.

In the end, I stop on a particular journalist's account, a guy who wrote an in-depth dissection of Fuchs and the awful shit he's done. Arne was so mad about that he couldn't even speak for several days. I'd been sent off to find any dirt about the journalist, anything Fuchs could use to hurt him.

I found some things, but I told Arne I didn't. It was one of the few times I disappointed him.

That journalist might be the best person to hear what I have to say. He works for Logan's wife though, and she hasn't forgotten what I did or forgiven me for it. Her eyes when I came down those stairs yesterday morning...

No, I can't go to him. Not at first.

I find another journalist, one who writes for a prestigious East Coast paper. He's done some interesting tech stuff, a story or two on electronic surveillance in other countries. So I message him, giving him the general outline of what I have. I don't say who I am or that I work for Corvus. And I pray like hell that Fuchs hasn't cracked the encryption on this particular secure messaging app.

My heart pounds for a long time after I hit Send. I've taken a big step here. A frightening one.

But it had to be done. I didn't steal all that data to keep it to myself. I stole it to give it to the world. To let them know what Corvus was doing to them in secret.

I wipe my hands on my sweatpants, then go upstairs to put the e-reader back where I found it. Elliot wouldn't be happy to know I've used the internet without his permission. And I need to keep my access secret so I can keep using it.

I've got the last book back in place, the e-reader hidden deep in the cupboard, when there's a knock at the door.

I slam the cupboard shut. My breath is coming too fast, my skin blooming with cold sweat. It's not Elliot—he wouldn't knock—so it must be the guards. And something's happened.

With small, steady steps, I make my way down the stairs. I force my face to assume my Minerva mask. Emotionless. Blank.

Inside, I'm anything but. If something's happened to Elliot… If he was hurt because he's helping me…

I cock my head, peer out the tiny window set in the door.

There's a woman outside. Something about her is familiar.

It takes me a moment to remember who she is—the office manager. She works for Bastard Capital. Except she's more than an office manager. Her position for them is more like mine was for Arne.

I open the door a crack and say nothing. I doubt it's a trick, but I can't be too careful.

"Elliot sent me." The woman's voice is strained, like she doesn't want to be here. "He told me to tell you that the code word is sleep."

That's what he told me to do last night, when he was holding me and I was too keyed up to relax.

She reaches into a bag. "And I've got your drive." She holds it up.

I wrench open the door then reach for it. I don't care if I'm being rude or graceless—I've given up too much for that thing to care.

"I have some things for you." She holds up the bag. "I'm Anjie, by the way."

I realize I haven't said a single word. "Minerva. But you know that."

"I do." She takes half a step toward the doorway. "Can I come in?"

I fall back, let her inside. "It's Elliot's home, not mine."

She brushes past me on the way to the kitchen/living area. "It's nice of him to let you stay here." Her eyes narrow as she turns to face me. "Most people don't realize it, but Elliot is a really good guy."

Ah, I'm being warned. *He kisses like a bad boy*, I'm tempted to say. "I haven't done anything to him."

She watches me for a long moment. "But you did things to other people. People close to him."

I cross my arms. "And now I'm going to expose those things—and Arne Fuchs—to the entire world."

"But you still did them."

I did. And there's no way out of that.

"Did Elliot send you here to tell me that?" I ask pointedly.

One perfect eyebrow rises. All of her is perfect, polished to a high vintage gleam. "I don't know what you said or did to get him to believe you, but the rest of us aren't fooled."

"Right." I raise my own eyebrows. "Because you guys just loved me before."

She shoves the bag at me. "Just so we understand each other. This isn't a truce."

"Oh, I completely understand." I take the bag at the last moment, almost when she's about to drop it.

"There're clothes and toiletries and food in there." She stalks to the door, her heels sharp on the hardwood floor. "And we've made a copy of that drive. In case you were thinking of selling it to anyone. We'll hear about it. And we'll stop you."

"Since I'm not doing that, knock yourself out."

She spins dramatically, her full skirt flaring out. "And don't even think about messing with Elliot."

I almost laugh because it's like we've entered an episode of *Dynasty*. But she's deadly serious.

They all love Elliot. Everyone at Bastard Capital. He's stiff and difficult and not just with me... but they love him. They're protecting him.

My amusement dies.

"Elliot can hold his own," I say with quiet seriousness.

"And all I want to do is get in touch with my friends. Then you'll never see or hear from me again."

"Good." There's a touch of vicious pleasure there. "Elliot said he'll be back this afternoon."

Something lightens in my chest. He didn't say that he was leaving me all alone here, under guard, but I did have the suspicion that he might. It would have been the logical thing to do.

But he's coming back. He's not deserting me.

"I'll see him then." I hug the bag to my chest. "And thank you for bringing these."

I'm so giddy over Elliot coming back that I'm actually being polite to this woman. Minerva would have never done that.

But I don't have to be her anymore.

CHAPTER 14

"Minerva?" I call into the darkened houseboat. "Minerva?"

It's only four in the afternoon, but the house is dark and quiet. I nodded to the security guys as I came in and they nodded back, so she hasn't escaped. But the house feels very empty.

It's ridiculous because my house is always empty until I come home. I'm the only one here.

"Minerva?" My heart is starting to pound. If she somehow slipped out, past the guards—or worse, Fuchs slipped in—

"I'm here." Her voice is weak as it floats down from the bedroom. Like she was asleep. Or sick.

I take the stairs two at a time.

She's in bed, the covers up to her chin, her face white, skin clammy. Two bright spots of red stain her cheeks.

"Sorry," she croaks. "But I think I have a fever."

I put my hand to her forehead and jump at the heat there. Jesus, she's on fire. "Yeah, you do. You must have caught something from being out in that storm."

"You don't catch a cold from being cold," she mumbles, her eyes half-closed.

Sick as she is and she still has to argue with me. It's… it's kind of endearing. There's a smile tugging at my mouth.

"Maybe so. But you're definitely sick."

"No doctor." With a mighty effort, she grabs my arm. Her hand is small, the bones and tendons delicate. But she holds on tight. "I can't trust any of them."

I agree that taking her to the doctor would be dangerous, but that fever feels nasty. Can't a person have a seizure if their temp gets too high?

I don't know. I don't know anything about taking care of a sick person because I've never had to do it before. It's a weighty responsibility.

"I should take your temperature." I look around as if a thermometer will magically appear. "Except there's no thermometer."

Or aspirin or ibuprofen or chicken soup or anything that might make her feel better. I've lived alone for so long that I've left all that behind.

"Don't need a thermometer. I'm not dying."

I'm not convinced of that. Her skin is so hot, her cheeks so red.

I put my hand to her forehead again, as if I can take a reading that way. She turns into my touch.

"Mmm, that feels good. Cool."

An idea hits me. "Wait here."

"Okay." She laughs a little wildly, as if I've told a joke and she's delirious from the fever.

I get a washcloth, soak it in the coldest water I can. I wring it out until it's just damp. I want it to be cool, not wet.

When I come back in, she's waiting, her eyes fully closed. She might be asleep, but there's something restless in her that tells me she's awake. Awake and too uncomfortable to truly sleep.

Carefully I lay the cloth on her forehead. She makes a deep noise of appreciation.

"Better?"

She nods. "I'll be okay once I get some sleep."

"But you can't sleep." She couldn't last night either, when she was well. I felt her moving in the bed, all through the night. She'd go still for a bit, then start tossing again.

"I slept the first day," she says. "I never do that. Or at least not when I was Minerva."

My entire body goes tense. Does she even know what she just said?

"I wondered what you were doing up there," I say slowly. "It was very quiet."

"I worked eighty-hour weeks," she says. "There wasn't time to sleep, much less sleep in. He doesn't sleep, you know."

I scoff. "He's not a vampire. I don't believe that."

Her expression darkens. "Whatever you've heard about him, it's all true. I promise."

I've heard a lot of crazy shit about Arne Fuchs. Most of it I don't believe. "The blood thing? Is that true?"

Her eyes open. "The blood thing? That's what you want to know about?"

"To begin with." If she's in a talking mood, I'm going to listen.

"Yes, it's true. Once a week he gets a blood transfusion from a young, healthy donor."

I can't help the way my lips pull away from my teeth. "Like a blood bag?" I'm picturing some kind of postapocalyptic scene with a tube connecting Fuchs to some young kid, blood flowing from the kid to him.

"The donor isn't there," she says. "But it's still pretty creepy."

"Wait, you had to be in there with him?" Someone might consider a medical procedure to be private. I certainly would.

"I was always with him. I had to be waiting outside his bedroom when he dressed, and I couldn't leave until he was back in his bedroom at night."

"But you said he didn't sleep."

"He still showered, changed his clothes. And there was the housekeeper…"

Now that was the other rumor I wanted to hear about it. "So that's true too."

She licks her lips. Shit, she's probably going to need some lip balm. Another thing I don't have. "I never saw them together," she says. "But there was definitely an odd current between them." Her gaze meets mine. "A spark."

The spark between *us* buzzes hard, bright.

I clear my throat because she's sick as all hell and I can't be thinking about those lips and the skin beneath her clothes.

"You changed." I shouldn't be surprised, but I kind of miss my clothes on her.

"Anjie brought some things." Minerva's tone is flat. She must not have liked the clothes.

I sit halfway on the bed, keeping some distance between us. "I can get you some other stuff. And I'll need to pick up some medicine. And chicken soup."

"Oh yeah." She blinks like she just remembered something. "That's what you eat when you're sick."

"Did you not know that?" My childhood wasn't the greatest, but I did get soup when I was sick.

"I did. But illness isn't allowed at Corvus. Especially for me."

It's one of the more common policies at tech companies: you can take as many sick days as you want officially, but unofficially you can't take a single day off. Work, work, and work some more—anyone who can't keep up with that gets shamed into doing it anyway.

I've never understood it even though I like to work hard myself. There's slacking off and then there's being sick. My dad was the ultimate slacker, which is why I can't stand laziness. But being ill is part of being human.

"You can't stop people from getting sick," I say. "Even if you're Arne Fuchs."

"You'd be amazed what symptoms you can suppress when you have to." She sighs. "Like appendicitis."

"What? No." That's not possible, even for her.

She nods. "I had to sneak into the ER at San Francisco General one night, get them to discharge me the next morning. He never once suspected." She says it like it was a tricky work assignment that she barely turned in on time. Not fun, but not that interesting.

"Jesus," I breathe. I know she's done bad things for Corvus, but I never really thought about what it would cost her to keep working there.

"Yep. Got a nice new scar. To go with all the ones nobody can see." She laughs that wild, high laugh again. "Might as well lay it all out. I'm fucked no matter what."

It's wrong to take advantage of her illness, but I want to hear this. More than my next breath. So I lean over, close enough to see the tiny lines under her eyes, the flutter of her pulse in her throat.

"Who are you? How did you end up here?"

"I never finished college." She smiles dreamily. "Are you shocked? I dropped out to do this."

"But your résumé..." I close my mouth on the rest of it. "Minerva went to UCSD. Not you."

"We had such big ideas. Ideals. College was a waste. The real world was calling."

"You and your friends?"

"It was Deena's idea. That we infiltrate a company, expose the immoral things it was doing. And Corvus was worst of all."

"So why didn't Deena do it?"

"I was the steady one. The best actress. But we didn't know what it would cost. A year to us then was nothing. But five years of that..." Her voice catches on a sob.

I take her hand, hold tight. Her skin isn't as hot as it once was. It's like the fever is draining as she confesses all this.

"You did an amazing thing," I say, close to her ear.

"All those people died because of me." Her breath is coming in jerky sobs.

Chills run over my skin. "What do you mean?"

She doesn't hear me. "I didn't want to do it, but I had to. I had to keep collecting and collecting, gathering all the evil things he made me do. That was what I was supposed to do there, and I did it. But none of you believe me." She's crying in earnest now, tears slipping down her cheeks. My heart is too heavy in my chest. "Anjie was…" Minerva rubs at her eyes. "It doesn't matter. I deserve it."

I don't think she does, actually. And it sounds like Anjie had some words with her, which is what Anjie would do. She's very protective of us.

But Minerva needs protecting too. "I believe you."

She's done awful things for Fuchs, and she probably should have left Corvus long before now—but she gave five years of her life to get that information. And her identity too. She's paid a high price for all of it.

Her hand drops. I'm still holding the other one. Her cheeks are paler, more rose than red. She looks almost soft.

"I didn't mean to dump all this on you." I realize she's apologizing. She insults me, then laughs and bares her soul, then apologizes. I don't know what to make of it. Or her. Or how it makes me feel. "I only wanted to contact my friends, then get out of here. Not get pushed onto the tracks or get sick or…" She bites her lip. "None of it was supposed to be like this."

"Leaving him was never going to be easy. And I'm glad I was there to save you." I can't help it; I press my lips to the back of her hand. Because I'm so, so glad I was there. "You should get some sleep. We can talk later."

"I'll be fine in a bit." Her voice is slurry with sleep. "Really, I just need a nap."

Nap sounds short. She needs way more sleep than that.

"Minerva, if you get up, I'm dragging you back to bed."

Her eyes stay closed as she smiles. "Caveman. And that's not my name."

I go still as stone. Again, does she know what she's saying? What she's giving away?

"Oh?" It's all I can manage without sounding too eager. I don't want to scare her into silence.

"It's Emily." She turns deeper into the pillow. Her mouth purses once, twice, and then a relaxed stillness steals over her.

She's asleep. Finally.

As quietly as I can, I fish my phone from my back pocket. Before I can think better of it, I fire off a text to Finn.

Her real name is Emily.

CHAPTER 15

He's feeding me soup.

Soup and toast and even a bowl of fruit, like I'm some kind of invalid. True, I feel like hell, but the kind of hell that could get up and feed myself.

When I suggested that, Elliot gave me a dark look, then held the spoon to my lips. "Your hands are trembling. And whenever you sit up too long, you start panting. Now eat."

I open my mouth for another bite. It's soup from a can, the chicken cut into too-perfect cubes and the broth the yellow of a crayon, but it still tastes good. And the toast is sourdough, way fancier than the soup.

"That's better," he says. "If you argued less, it'd make things easier."

I open my mouth to point out that I haven't been arguing at all the past few hours—I've been asleep—but he shoves the spoon back in my mouth.

The twitch of his mouth tells me it was intentional, to keep me from talking.

He's not sweet. Our time together has revealed that he's short and surly and he's helping me against his better sense. The way he's lifting the spoon to my mouth isn't exactly gentle—it's more efficient than anything. *Food goes into the mouth, get it in there* I can picture him thinking.

But there's care in him. It's rough, but it's there.

"Enough," I say between bites. "Thank you."

He lifts a napkin, pats my lips. "You sure? There's more."

I nod quickly because he's got a look like he'll keep going until the bowl is empty. "I'm full."

He sets the napkin on the lap tray. I'm propped up in his bed, the tray of food across my lap, and he's sitting next to me, leaning over me. He smells clean, fresh, like he just got out of the shower.

I can't smell that good, not when I've been sweating out a fever for hours.

"Eat a few bites of fruit," he orders.

He really is a bossy asshole. If I say no, I already know what he'll respond with: "It's good for you and you need your strength back." And then he'll give me that lawyerly look, the one that says I can't argue my way out of that one.

I like his bossy-asshole side. It makes me want to argue with him.

I used to love arguing with men. Give me a man who'd debate me for hours on just about anything, and I'd be panting with lust by the end. And not stupid "I'm the man so I'm right" arguing. Real, deep arguments. A matching of wits.

A fight over fruit isn't a battle of minds, so I take a bite of some melon. But I'm tempted to give him some sass regardless.

Minerva didn't sass anyone. She gave orders, threats. You didn't argue with her because she had the upper hand in any situation.

I dreamed that I told him my real name. And that he said it soft and slow, rolling it in his mouth like rare winter fruit.

I'm also worried that I didn't dream it. That I really told him. Things were fuzzy in that fever before he made me take some ibuprofen.

I take another bite—a blueberry this time—then ask, "Is this enough?"

He peers into the bowl, giving me a view of the top of his head. His hair is thick, dark, a touch longer than I would have expected. It's got waves, and it looks like he's run his hands through it several times today.

"I suppose that's good." Oh boy, Mr. Grudging.

"I try," I say dryly.

He pins me with a dark look. "You're feeling better."

"Wasn't that the point?" If he wanted me dead, there are better ways to do it. Like leaving me on the Caltrain tracks.

He doesn't answer. Instead, he takes the tray and sets it aside, all without getting off the bed. He's graceful for such a reserved man. No poker up the ass for him.

"Uh-oh," he says when he catches sight of my flushed cheeks. He leans over, pulling the comforter tight over my thighs. Pinning me down. "Is your fever coming back?"

I can't dodge his hand quick enough. When his palm finds my forehead, it's like jumper cables directly to my heart. I'm too sick to be reacting like this, but my libido didn't get the message.

"Feels okay," he says to himself. "And you have an hour and twenty-three minutes before you can take more medicine."

And there it is again, that care that's unique to him. I bet he has a timer set on his phone just so he doesn't dose me a minute sooner than the bottle says.

"I'm fine," I say. Mostly to get him to move his hand.

He lifts his palm but doesn't move any farther. "We were talking before you fell asleep."

Oh shit. I wasn't dreaming it. "About what?" Maybe I can fake not remembering.

"Knock it off." His tone is sharp enough to make me flinch. "Stop pretending."

I swallow hard. "I thought I might have dreamed it."

"You didn't." His voice isn't as cold, but it's still hard. "What did you mean about killing all those people?"

"I don't remember that." At his look, I say, "I don't. Honestly. I thought I told you— I don't remember that. I told you about the blood transfusions and the housekeeper, right?"

He nods. Good, I'm not going completely crazy. "You also said something about killing some people. You were crying."

I stare at the far wall. I haven't cried… for years. The first year, yes. I'd come home and cry to myself. And then I just sort of… turned it off. Turned completely into Minerva.

"It's a facial-recognition program." I can't look at him as I tell him this. Minerva would have gloated about it. "There were several authoritarian governments that were interested. They wanted to track down dissidents. So… we did that for them, to demonstrate how powerful it was. A group of feminists here, a religious minority there, a troublesome ethnic group everywhere. We tracked down every name and picture they gave us, told them where to find those people." I pick at the coverlet. The stitches are tight, good quality. They don't budge. "Those people all disappeared. Every single one that we found."

He doesn't say anything, which I'm grateful for. I want to sit with what I've done. I don't want to hear that it will be okay, that if I didn't do it, someone else would.

Someone else didn't do it—I did. I justified it by telling myself that I'd expose it to the world and stop it, but those people are all still gone.

Finally I glance over at Elliot. His head is bent and I can't see his expression. He's appalled. He must be. Lawyers have a reputation for being slimy, but he's the furthest thing from slimy. He's like a knight of old, all upstanding with his code of honor and his shield and sword of the law.

"We sold it to the FBI actually," I say to the top of his

head. "So that'll be the thing they use to bring me in when all this is done."

He lifts his head and his eyes… I gasp and rear back.

He's *furious*.

As I watch him, I realize it's not focused on me. That anger is aimed at something past me.

"He'll fucking do anything, won't he?"

It takes me a moment to realize Elliot's talking about Fuchs.

"I helped him do it."

Elliot inhales, his anger fading. "Yeah, but the panopticon, the spyware, killing dissidents—he pursues all that. And for what? How much more money does he need? He's ruining lives so he can add another billion to his bank account."

I shake my head. "It's not about the money. It's power. He's already bought everything he wants, which honestly isn't much." Arne never flashed his wealth. After the first few billion, I don't think he even kept track. "But having a government—an entire government—under your thumb? That's what he wants. Governments, people, the entire world: he wants it all under his control."

Elliot's hand curls into a fist on the coverlet. It's only inches from my thigh. "You shouldn't have worked on the facial-recognition program," he says. He's quiet, serious. "But Fuchs is evil. There's more than enough blame to go around." When he looks at me again, it spears me, but in a different way. "You're not evil. I thought you were, but you're not."

"Not evil doesn't mean innocent."

"No."

I exhale, my lungs emptying in a relieved rush. That's what I need to hear. Not that I'm a good person, that what I did was okay in the end… but that I'm not completely irredeemable. Coming from him, a person who used to think I was evil, makes it mean so much more.

"Thank you." I put all my sincerity in my gaze. I… I open myself to him. Even the bad parts. Especially the bad parts.

He shrugs one shoulder. It should be dismissive, but on him, since he's so reserved, it's endearing. Like he's feeling too raw to give a full shrug. "Are you feeling better?"

So we're done with my confessions. It's good, because I'm suddenly exhausted. Completely drained. But in a good way.

"Yeah. Thanks for the food. And feeding me."

His fist on the coverlet opens. His fingers are long, thick, his palm broad. It's a hand that would have fit well on a farmer or a construction worker. Someone needing strength to get through their day-to-day work. It fits him well too.

"No problem." He ducks his head, clears his throat. "You've had a rough time." When he gets up from the bed, the pressure on my thighs releases. "I'll take care of the tray. Do you want to sleep more?"

A question instead of an order. I guess all I had to do to soften him up was bare my deepest, darkest secrets. "I think I will."

He nods. "Call me if you need anything. I'll just be downstairs."

I'm tempted to ask if he'll be sleeping up here again. But I don't. "Thanks."

And then he's gone.

CHAPTER 16

When I wake up the next morning—thirteen hours of sleep, a new record for me—I immediately know that Elliot hasn't been in the bed. The coverlet is neatly tucked around me, no wrinkles, and I'm smack-dab in the middle of the bed. No room even on the edges for a big, surly, handsome-as-hell lawyer.

I'm not disappointed. I just feel bad that he had to sleep on the couch again.

Before I go down to see him though… I cock my head and listen for any movement from downstairs. It's quiet. Completely so. Looks like Elliot doesn't snore.

As stealthily as I can, I slip out of bed and start going through the book cabinet. I pull out the e-reader carefully, not making a single noise. I've even stopped breathing.

I switch it on, wait impatiently for it to power up. *Come on, come on, come on.*

I glance at the stairs, but it's still quiet. Just needs to stay like that until I check my email.

The email window pops up. Quickly I scroll through, but there's nothing from Deena. I shouldn't feel abandoned—I was gone for five years, and it's only been a few days since I contacted her—but I do. It's also sadness about Reagan. Just a bad mix.

And then I come across the next email. *Interested. Pls send more.*

It's from the journalist. And he wants to see some of what I have so he can verify it.

I set the e-reader down and stare at the message. It's a sign. My friends aren't answering, but the journalist is.

I have to go it alone. The way I have been the entire time.

Except I can't access the drive. Not from this rinky-dink e-reader. Crap. I'm going to need Elliot's laptop.

But he's not going to leave me alone with it. I'm going to have to come up with some excuse to look at the drive, then send something to the journalist without Elliot knowing. It can be done, but I'll have to think about how to make it happen.

First I need a shower. I've been sweating out this sickness, and I'm sticky with it. Ugh.

The shower products Anjie brought over smell amazing. I can feel the ickiness washing away. I feel human again.

There's lotion too and some face cream and a comb. When I'm done, my skin is bare and clean, my hair still wet but long and loose. It's almost like I've been reborn.

But I'm not one hundred percent well. My head holds the echo of a headache, and my limbs are weak. But my head is clear. And I'm starving for something beyond soup. So I'm heading downstairs.

I go through the clothes Anjie brought, looking for something comfortable. Most of what she included is what I would have worn as Minerva—structured suits, severe dresses, tailored pants. None of which I want to wear now.

But she also put in some pajamas and yoga gear. I wore a slouchy shirt and yoga pants while I was sick, which have to be washed now, but there should be something similar in there.

The second my hand closes on the silky fabric, I know this is the one. It turns out to be a set of jewel-blue pajamas, menswear style, but in a slick, slinky fabric that's decadent beyond words. Everything will be covered, but when it's covered by something like this...

These pajamas might be too suggestive, but after everything I've been through, I want to feel pretty and comfortable. Besides, I'm not going to taunt Elliot about his cock in my mouth, so he won't be tempted to kiss me.

I take a moment to check out my reflection before I head down. The blue makes my eyes take on gold tones, and the dark brown of my hair doesn't look so boring. I never wore colors like this when I was Minerva, and seeing myself in them again... it gets me a little choked up.

Before I can completely dissolve into tears, I go downstairs.

Elliot is laid out on the couch. There's no other way to describe it. He's on his stomach, one leg hanging off, looking like he fell face-first into that position. He's definitely not reserved or controlled when he sleeps. He's in a T-shirt and sweats and...

I do a double take. I think that's the exact shirt and pants I was wearing earlier. But maybe not.

The last step creaks when my foot hits it. Elliot snaps upright, his eyes wide.

I stop. "Sorry. I didn't mean to scare you."

He blinks, pushing himself to a sitting position. "I'm not scared."

"Oh, excuse me. Startled."

He gives me a look that says he doesn't appreciate the sarcasm. Probably needs to wake up a little more before he can fully savor it.

"How are you feeling?" He runs his hands through his hair as he asks, pushing it away from his face. It falls in deep waves, almost curls.

"Um." It's hard not to focus on his hair. And his fingers running through it. "Fine. I had a shower, and I feel much better." I point up to the bathroom through the ceiling. "You probably heard me."

I'm babbling. Why am I babbling? I never used to do this, not ever. He loosens something in me.

Elliot grunts as he pushes up off the couch. "I did. What time is it?" He checks his watch, which manages to be both sleek and heavy.

The curtains are closed, but I can see through the cracks that the sky is dark. I must have slept all evening.

My stomach rumbles. Of course he hears it.

"I guess it's dinnertime." He walks into the kitchen, blocking my path to the living room. "I have more soup."

I make a face. "Can I get something more... real?"

"Soup is good for you." He pulls out a can.

"Are you a doctor now?"

"You just can't stop arguing, can you?" he growls.

I sit down on the step. "I don't think there's any real evidence that soup cures anything. And I'm feeling better anyway."

His mouth flattens. He's probably pondering force-feeding me again. "How about some grilled cheese?"

"You can make that?" At his look, I say quickly, "It sounds amazing."

As he assembles and cooks it, he keeps glancing at me. "You got new clothes."

There's a deep undercurrent in his voice that snares my attention. "Yeah. Anjie brought them."

He looks like he wants to say more. Instead, he just keeps stealing glances every chance he gets. It's... nice. He was attracted to me before, back when he hated me, but this is different. Purer.

I'm not going to encourage it, but I can enjoy it. And I can enjoy watching him as he works. His loose clothes can't hide the strength and grace in his body. He flips the sandwich with practiced motions, carefully checking the browning on each side. He's serious about his grilled cheese.

"If it burns, I'll eat it and make you a new one," he says. "You're watching me like you're worried."

"No." I hug my knees to my chest. I'm not the only one caught looking it seems. "You're my only entertainment."

He snorts. "Poor you." He slides the sandwich on a plate, hands it to me. "Go sit at the table."

I do, tearing into the sandwich as he makes himself one. It's delicious, hot and gooey with just the right amount of crispy butteriness. After a day spent sick in bed, it's the perfect recipe for recovery.

He eats his sandwich at the counter, which is a slight disappointment. But I understand that he wants his space. I've invaded here, and he's used to being alone.

"Thanks," I say as I carry my plate to the sink. "For all of it."

He finishes off his last bite. "I'm not used to taking care of somebody who's sick."

"I'm not used to being sick." I take a seat on the couch, tucking one leg under my butt. "I need to access my drive."

I've decided to tackle the issue head-on. The drive belongs to me and I can use it. Simple as that.

He goes stiff. "I can't let you do that."

"What?" I get up, grab the drive. It's been sitting between us on the coffee table the entire time. "It's mine."

"So go ahead." He props a hip against the countertop, lifts a lazy hand. "Open it up. No one's stopping you."

"Very funny. You know I need your laptop to do it. Which you won't give me."

He cocks his head in acknowledgment. "We can't let you back into that drive."

We?

Ah, the Bastards told him not to let me touch it. When he

went in today, they all put their heads together and schemed on this. About thwarting me.

I'm the one who went to all the trouble to get the data, but being typical, insufferable assholes, they've decided they're the ones who own it.

"So what do you have planned for *my* data? Do I at least get to know?"

"Nothing's planned." He walks over, puts a large hand over the drive. "No one's done anything with it."

"Right. The rest of them weren't salivating with glee at the thought of punishing me. You certainly were."

The gleam in his eyes stops my breath. "You want to be punished."

I pull the drive into my chest, trapping his hand between my breasts. "I do not. I want my drive."

"Liar." His warm breath washes over my face. He flexes his hand and I gasp. "That's why you came to me."

"No," I protest even as I lift my chest, pressing his hand deeper into me. I'm on fire, my sex aching, and he's hardly even touched me. It's been so long, but it's also *him*. It's mostly him.

With an easy tug, he takes the drive from me. Like taking a toy from a kid, it's so simple. But the darkness behind his eyes keeps me from protesting.

He grabs my hip, drags me into him. His eyes are dark, fathomless, his face tense. Like he hates himself for doing this.

I'd say I know the feeling, but that's not hate coursing through me. It's white-hot, molten, but it's more like frustration. And it's drawing me like a magnet to him.

"I don't want this." His breath is coming in harsh pulls, his hand tight on my waist. "I don't want you. But God help me, I can't stop."

"I know." I run my hands down his chest, thick with muscle. And hair—it's springy under my palms, like it wants to get at me as much as I want to get at it. "I don't want this either."

He lowers his head and kisses me. There's no gentleness, only hunger. Desperation. His tongue thrusts into my mouth and I moan.

This isn't punishment, but it's exactly what I wanted. What I needed.

I fist my hands in his shirt, needing to get it off. All those stupid suits he wears, looking so starchy and sexy, and then coming at me in a plain T-shirt? He meant to drive me insane with lust.

He helps me get it over his head, releasing me for the barest moment. And then he's on me again, devouring me with deep, drugging kisses. He's consuming me, burning away anything that isn't pure lust.

I run my hands over his stomach, his sides, his chest. There's hair everywhere, which I love. He's bound up in three-piece gray tweed all day, and underneath is *this*. Wild, feral hair and muscles and hot skin. The next time I see him in a suit, I might just tear it off him.

One of his hands cups my jaw. His touch is firm, anchoring. He's not worried about breaking me. Probably because he knows what I've already survived.

His other hand starts to unbutton my pajama top. The buttons slip free with the lightest touch, sliding over the silk as if barely held in place. My breasts are tight, aching, and every rasp of my breath rubs my nipples against that hard wall of chest.

When the last button is free, he lifts his head and jerks the top down, letting it fall from his hand. "Jesus." His chest is rising and falling, the tendons in his neck stark. "I love your tits."

I almost laugh, because *tits*? Really? "You are the last person I'd expect to call them tits."

Honestly, they're not my favorite feature. Too small, with

dark, prominent nipples. If they were bigger, with pinker, shyer nipples, I wouldn't mind so much.

He frowns fiercely as he takes them in both hands. "They're more beautiful than I even imagined."

I swallow hard because he's playing with my nipples, teasing them into diamond-hard points, and *beautiful?* And *imagined?*

"You hate me," I whisper. It's a terrible thought to have in the moment, but I can't help it.

He shakes his head. "Not now."

I don't know if he means only while he's holding my breasts or if he means generally now. And then I don't care, because he takes one nipple in his mouth.

He's bending down to me, suckling me, and it's amazing. Glorious. He tugs, and every inch of me pulses. But especially in my pussy. That's becoming one sustained pulse, all this overflow of sensation gathering there.

I press my thighs tight together, increasing the pressure. Oh God, but that's good. I run my fingers through his hair, holding on. It's amazingly soft, and the waves curl around my fingers, tangling me in him.

My heart swells with something I can't name at the sight of my hand in his hair.

He moves to my other breast, giving it the same careful, detailed attention. He licks this way, sucks that way, varies speed and pressure, until I'm delirious with it. Who knew he was so inventive?

I squeeze my thighs together again. Holy crap, I'm already close, just from him playing with my nipples. That's never happened before.

He lifts his head, frowns at me. Man, I never would have thought a frown could be devastating like a smile, but his are. "What's wrong? You got tense."

Heat crawls up my cheeks. "I was... I needed some pressure."

A small, wicked smile curves his lips. "Oh do you?"

He cups me outside my pants, his palm barely grazing my clit. Even that faint touch has me close to exploding. He presses the crotch of my panties into my folds, using the fabric to caress me.

"So hot," he murmurs. "Are you wet too?"

I loop my arms around his neck because otherwise I'm going to fall. I manage to nod.

"How wet?" He rubs harder. "I want details."

Bossy, bossy, bossy. And way filthier than I was expecting. "Pretty wet. I'm… I'm going to soak through these panties soon."

His smile is all sharp triumph. "I bet I can make it happen sooner." His thumb finds my clit and strums.

My knees give out as lightning stitches through me. My clit was already swollen, aching, and he's just applied a current straight to it.

"Hey." His arm wraps around my waist, catching me. But he doesn't let up on my clit. "Careful."

A snappy remark; that's what I'm reaching for, but I can't find one. Seriously, my brain can only produce something like *Ungh*. Not at all snappy.

"I'm fine," I say, although I'm clearly not. My shirt is gone, my legs aren't working, and if he doesn't touch my bare pussy in the next two seconds, I'm going to implode. This over-the-clothes tease is killing me.

He gets the point, touching the skin of my belly first. I gasp, my stomach pulling tight. It's like sparks of heat dancing between him and me. Like magic.

And then his hand slips lower. He goes slow, his eyes locked tight with mine.

There's amazement, wonder in his gaze. He's not going slow to torment me—he's going slow because he's enjoying the discovery so much.

When his fingers find my folds, I release a long exhale. He does too.

"You're so fucking wet." It's praise and shock all at once.

I feel inordinately pleased, although I haven't really done anything. It's all him.

"So wet," he whispers again, fingering me with exquisite awareness. "And hot. And soft."

He pushes one finger, then two inside me. His fingers twist in some tricky way, and I moan, shoving myself against his hand.

When he pulls his fingers out of me, I whimper, my arms tightening around his neck. "No." Normally I'd be appalled at how needy I sound, but I'm beyond caring.

"Shhh." He puts his fingers in his mouth, licks off my taste. "I had to know. Couldn't stop thinking about it."

This man needs to come with a warning because he's deadly. I'm amazed I didn't come right then. But I'm close. So close.

"Beautiful," he says again, putting his hand back where I need it. This time he finds my clit too, stroking it in time with his fingers thrusting inside me.

It's too much. My body is going to tear itself apart.

His cock presses hard on my belly as his fingers work in my pussy. He thrusts once, twice, in time with the motions of his hand.

I grab his hair, seal my mouth to his. His cock is fucking my belly, his fingers are fucking my pussy, and my tongue is fucking his mouth. It's all so goddamn *raw.*

He releases my waist, grabbing my knee and hooking it over his hip, opening me even more to him. The rhythm of his hand on my sex never slows though. He's not giving me even an inch to breathe, to slow down. He's making this climax come for me as hard as it can.

When it does come, every muscle in me clenches at the

power of it. Even my toes. Strange noises come between my clenched teeth, animal things that I hardly recognize.

Elliot holds me the entire time. He strokes slower, gentler, like he's helping me come down. It's… it feels sweet, even though I know he's not.

It makes me feel sweet, even though I know I'm not.

Finally I gain control of my limbs, although I'm still limp. I haven't come that hard since… since ever.

Elliot's watching me closely, the lines around his mouth strained. His chest is gloriously bare, and lower… My eyes widen.

I reach for his erection straining at his waistband. All I can think about is him filling me, easing the emptiness in the heart of me. My orgasm is fading and I still need more. More of him.

He grabs my hand before I touch him. His touch is firm, letting me know that he's not kidding around. "No. Just you."

I don't understand, then I do. He can touch me, bring me to an intense climax, but I can't do the same for him.

It could be read as him being nice to me, putting my pleasure first, but it doesn't feel that way. I thought we were in this together, but I was wrong.

I wriggle my wrist free. "You don't have to—"

He turns his head. "I do. And you need your rest."

"You weren't so concerned about my health when I was screaming your name as I came a few minutes ago."

His gaze flares red-hot, and for a moment I think he might grab me and toss me down on the sofa. Finish this the way we both want it to.

But slowly, his cheek twitching, he brings all that fire back under his control. He reaches down, brings up my pajama shirt. "Put this on."

I consider telling him "Make me," but the fight is draining out of me. As much as I hate to admit it, he's right—I'm crashing again. So instead I start to pull it on, my hands clumsy.

He sighs, then comes to help me. As quickly as he undid them, he's got the buttons closed again. For a moment his fingers seem to linger on the last button, the one closest to my throat, but then he releases it.

"Can you get into bed by yourself?" His cock is still hard and straining, tenting his pants. But he seems determined to ignore it, to deny his need.

Fine. He can play the martyr. I don't care.

He just gave me the best orgasm of my life, and I'm already furious with him again. That's quite the talent.

"I'm good. I'll see you in the morning."

I don't offer to share the bed or take the couch. I'm going to enjoy having that bed all to myself, all out of spite.

But holding my spite all night won't quite be the same as holding him.

"Have you found anything yet?"

I'm trying to keep my voice down as I talk to Finn over the phone, but voices carry in this tiny space. The stairs basically act as a noise funnel, which means Minerva can probably hear everything.

When I checked on her, she was asleep. But she could have been pretending. Or she could be awake now.

I'm too frustrated and wound up to care. I want to climb up the stairs, get into my own bed, and fuck her senseless. I also want to know who she really is and what else she's hiding.

I want my calm, staid life back too. I've got a hard-on like whoa, but I can't do anything about it, which was never a problem when I lived alone. This keeps up, I'm going to pass out from lack of blood.

So I called Finn. If he's found anything on Minerva, that should make me feel better. And being reminded of what a liar she is should help kill my erection.

"Dude," Finn says, "I don't have much to go on. I started by limiting the search to just California, but a woman named Emily who disappeared five years ago? You're still talking thousands of records to go through. Maybe even a million. It's a big state."

"I thought you were a genius at this." I want to smash my phone into my forehead.

"I am, but you need to chill. What, did you get into another fight with her? You sound tense."

Tense. That's hilarious. "I'm fine. I just need to know what you've found."

"Did you get her last name by any chance?"

"She, uh, she's been sick." And the minute she felt better, I fingered her like a horny teenager.

"Should have gone to a hotel," Finn says.

Which would have left Minerva ill and completely alone. "I'm good. I'll try again on the last name. What about the hard drive?"

"Oh." I *hear* Finn's eyes widening. "That shit is amazing. They've got this facial-recognition algorithm that's so fucking sick. Light-years ahead of anything I've seen before."

Great. So Minerva made a really great tool to oppress people. That won't add to her guilt at all.

"Don't tell her that," I say.

He misunderstands me. "Don't worry. I'm not going to compliment her."

I swallow my angry sigh. There's no point explaining how they're wrong about her. "She wants her drive back."

"I thought Anjie gave it to her."

"She did, but she's got no computer to access it. I told her I couldn't let her have my laptop. Do you know Dev's reasons for not letting her have her own data?"

There's a long silence. "I don't think she should have it either."

I work my jaw. I have to keep my voice down, but I really, really want to shout. "It's hers. What do you care if she stole it?"

"I don't. In fact, I'm stoked she did. But she can't sell this shit. It's too explosive. Did you know the CIA and the NSA are fighting over some of this stuff? That's crazy."

It is, and she's going to be caught in the middle. She already is. "So what do we do? You guys don't want to release it, but we can't keep her here forever."

"Wait, you want to give it back to her?"

I pace through the living room. The curtains are closed, so no one from outside can see me, but I still feel exposed. "I think she's going to give it to the press."

Finn bursts out with a laugh. "Is that what she told you? Man, I love you like a brother, but you're not seeing straight here."

"She gave you and Doc all that information. She helped get Doc's brother out of prison."

"And she helped put him there in the first place." Finn's getting angry now, a rare thing for him. "Are you arguing 'cause you believe her or because it's your favorite thing?"

I'm not going to get any further with Finn than I did with Logan. I need to try a more neutral party. "Sorry, can't help it. I haven't slept much."

"It'll all be over soon." Finn's typing something—I hear the clatter of the keyboard across the line. "We'll figure this thing out and then she'll be gone."

My mouth flattens. I don't want her gone, just disappeared into the world. Or worse, in a prison cell. But Finn's not going to understand. "Let me know if you find anything. Oh, and has there been anything else about this promotion story? Anything about how she's disappeared?"

"No. Fuchs is going to want to keep that nice and quiet. His favorite employee running off with all his secrets isn't a good look for him."

"Yeah. Thanks, man."

I hang up, then tap the phone against the couch arm. There's a tickle in the back of my throat like I've been talking too much and a tightness at my temples. Probably the symptoms of blue balls coming out.

I glance down at myself. At least my erection has died down. Although I'm still clenched up with need. She's so close. And she tasted...

I shake my head. This is madness. I need to focus on something else.

Like how everyone close to me keeps insisting that Minerva hasn't changed. The Bastards aren't saying it to piss me off, even though it feels that way. They're reminding me of what I shouldn't forget.

That Minerva has been my enemy—our enemy—for as long as we've known her. That she's deliberately hurt people close to us. Pretended to enjoy it even.

Hell, maybe she really did enjoy it. Did she keep up a role for five years... or did she just eventually fall so far into it there was no gap between who she was before and who she was pretending to be?

I need to get more out of her about her past. Keep my head clear around her and my mind on my mission.

But goddamn, those silky blue pajamas... I'd dare anyone to keep their head if she came out in those.

Actually, I don't. I want the sight of her in those pajamas to be all mine.

I'm fucked.

I brace my hands on the counter and let my head hang between my arms. But the rush of blood to my brain doesn't help.

So I pick up the phone and call Dev.

"Yes?" He never says hello. Just *yes*, as if he knew you were calling before the phone even rang.

"Minerva wants her drive back. And I'm thinking I'll give it to her."

I don't know why I'm taking the aggressive route immediately. Maybe it has to do with whatever I heard in Dev's voice at that meeting that I didn't like.

Maybe it's my sexual frustration working itself out on an innocent target.

"What does she want with it?"

That catches me up short. Her friends haven't contacted her—Finn's hacked into the email accounts she set up on my laptop and he's watching them—so why would she need the drive again? Just to look over all the stuff she took?

"She didn't say. But I'll ask her."

"You haven't given her any internet access, have you?"

"No. What the hell do you think she's going to do?" I'm starting to get pissed at Dev—she's not some criminal mastermind. "Why can't she access the drive?"

There's a long beat of silence. "She's already contacted a reporter. All she needs now is the drive and she can send him everything."

That's impossible. Dev doesn't know what he's talking about.

But Emily's crafty. Cunning. My stomach knots. "How do you know that?"

Dev doesn't answer. "Releasing that information now might be disastrous."

My skin goes cold. Dev is being very weird, even more than usual. "What are you doing? Is she going to get hurt?"

"No one's going to be hurt." His tone is calm. "And I need her to not blow everything apart. Just trust me."

I should. Dev's been with the Bastards from the very beginning. The algorithm that made us all billionaires—he wrote it. He might be the secretive one, but I'm the outsider. They didn't need a lawyer until after they got rich.

Being Logan's brother was my entrance into their world, not any special tech skills of mine. But they accepted me wholeheartedly anyway.

I need to listen to Dev and not my libido when it comes to Emily. But it's so goddamn tough.

"You're up to something," I say. "Do the others know?"

"Just keep her under control. Remember everything she's done. Remember who she works for."

"She's living in my house. I can't forget."

"What's she been doing this whole time?"

"Sleeping. She's sick," I explain.

"Really?" Dev seems surprised something so mundane could happen to her. "No more murder attempts?"

"No. But he has to know she's here." I pull aside the curtain, looking for the guards. One waves to me from the dock.

"He knows she can't stay there forever, so he can bide his time. It's what I'd do."

I frown at the approval in his voice. "Are you channeling him now or something?"

"He's not that mysterious. He's just willing to go further in pursuit of his goals than most people."

"Willing to cross more lines, you mean."

"That too," Dev agrees. "And she crossed those lines with him. Just because she's betrayed Fuchs doesn't mean she's suddenly innocent."

No. But things are generally more complicated than innocent and guilty, and things are super fucking complicated here.

A thought occurs to me. "Have you been trying to find her real name too?"

He makes a noncommittal noise. "If I find it, you'll be the first to know."

Which doesn't really answer the question of if he's looking, but Dev is a withholding bastard.

"But you're more likely to get it out of her first," he says. "Being stuck there with her."

It doesn't feel like being stuck. It's too comfortable, too intimate for that.

"I'm doing my best," I say, which isn't entirely true. I should be always pressing her, trying to get more. Trying to get the full truth from her.

Instead, I'm playing nurse and getting her off. If Dev knew, he'd be shocked. Disapproving.

Which isn't enough to make me feel guilty about it.

"Will you be in tomorrow?" Dev asks. "We can send over a nurse. And you can still get a hotel room."

"It's fine. Taking care of her…" My voice tries to fade, but I force it on. "It's fine. We'll survive."

Dev laughs softly. "Yeah, as long as you keep her away from the Caltrain."

"She's not going anywhere," I promise.

CHAPTER 18

I'm awakened by a groan. Or maybe it's a moan.

It's some noise of pain and it's five in the morning. I was sleeping so well too, dreaming of Elliot naked, cock rock hard, telling me how stupid he was to stop us earlier. How I'm always right. About everything.

It was a great dream.

The noise comes again. That's definitely a human, and they are not in good shape. And they're downstairs.

I stumble out of bed. It must be Elliot, but I can't think what's going on. The security detail hasn't come crashing in, so I don't think someone broke in.

"Elliot?" I flip on the kitchen light. "What's going on?"

He's on the couch again, but this time he's on his back. His shirt is still off—God help me—and one arm is tossed over his eyes. His skin gleams with a fine sheen of sweat.

In a moment I'm next to him. The heat coming off his skin shocks me.

"Oh no, you got sick too," I say as I kneel next to him.

"No," he mumbles.

I wriggle my hand under his arm to check his temperature. Oh yeah, he's burning up. Like, worrisomely hot.

He grabs my wrist, tosses it away. And bares his teeth.

Good Lord, someone's a bad patient. "You're definitely sick. And if you bite me, I'll bite you back."

"Promise?"

Oh, if he weren't so sick, I'd be so turned on by that. What a waste of a flirtatious remark.

"See?" I take his arm and pull him off the couch. "You don't get sick from being out in the cold. It's a virus."

I get him to his feet and he leans heavily on me, making me stagger.

"God, I wish I could make you stop arguing."

We stumble together toward the stairs. "I think you like it."

"Like isn't the word."

Implying that I inspire something beyond simple liking with my arguing. Something sexier.

Somehow we drag ourselves up the stairs. I manage to roll him into the bed, pull the coverlet out from under him, then tuck him in.

"I'll bring you some ibuprofen," I say. "And some 7UP."

He frowns. Sick as he is, it still hits me right in the chest. "7UP?"

"Yep. Didn't you get 7UP when you were sick?"

He shakes his head, his eyes closing. "There's no more chicken soup. No 7UP."

The sadness in his voice kills me. Like he can't imagine a world where he'd get soup and 7UP when he's sick. It might just be the fever talking—his skin is like a stove top—but the emotions feel real.

"I'll get you some ibuprofen and water then," I say. "We'll deal with the chicken soup and 7UP shortage later."

It doesn't take me long to go through the bathroom cabinets. Elliot is a minimalist for sure—there's a razor, shave cream, and some soap there, and not much else. The ibuprofen is front and center, and I fill the cup by the sink for him.

He takes the pills without complaining, then flops back onto the bed once he's done. He looks so miserable my heart wrings out. I want to do something more for him, besides the little I've done so far.

Chicken soup and 7UP. I can try to find that, have it ready for when he feels more like himself.

I head downstairs and start going through the kitchen cabinets. But… they're mostly empty. There are plates and cups and silverware and pots and pans, but anyone could own those. The things he might like—boxed mac 'n' cheese, a certain kind of cracker or cookie, or even a loaf of bread—aren't here.

Or maybe I've consumed all the food he had. Ate up the bread and the chicken noodle soup he likes. He gave everything he had in the cupboards to me.

I enjoy the thought. It warms me like a hot cup of cocoa. Which he also doesn't have.

My gaze falls on his briefcase, lingers over his laptop. I hold my breath.

This would be the perfect chance to plug in my drive and send everything to the journalist. I won't get another window like this.

But he's sick. Upstairs, all alone. Suffering. And he took care of me when I was in a similar state.

Reluctantly I turn away from the laptop. I can try again once he feels better.

First I need to get some food in this place. Real, nourishing food. And honey and tea. Everything I remember as being comforting when I was sick.

There's a grocery store just down the street. I could run down there and grab some things. Cans of soup, some tea, crackers—it would take ten minutes tops for me to grab all that. I'd be in and out before anyone saw me.

But grocery stores are filled with cameras. They'd see me.

I'm tempted, so tempted to sneak out to the grocery store.

I haven't done something so ordinary in years. And cooking… it's been so long. I used to love it, back before I was Minerva. I want to give Elliot something cooked by me, with affection.

I look again at his laptop. Next to it is his phone.

Delivery. The reason why I haven't been grocery shopping in forever is because I get groceries delivered. I don't need to go out—I can have it brought to me.

Except I don't have a credit card. Or cash. I need someone to help. The only person I can think who can…

I swallow hard. Anjie made it more than clear that she does not like me. She's not going to be pleased if I call her asking for a grocery delivery. I'd rather call anyone else but her.

Although there isn't anyone else. If I want to help Elliot, I need to swallow my pride.

When I pick up his phone, the home screen immediately comes up. He doesn't even have a password on it. Oh, Elliot. We really need to have a chat about IT security. But first…

I do an internal fist pump when I see his contacts list. There's Anjie, right there at the top. I hit the Call button.

While it rings, I run upstairs to check on Elliot. He's where I left him, in a restless sleep. His brow is knotted and his limbs are tense. As if he's physically fighting the illness, even in his sleep. Poor guy.

"Hey!" Anjie sounds so happy when she answers. "How are things?"

I clear my throat. "Uh, it's not Elliot. It's Em—Minerva."

"Oh." Anjie's voice drops into disappointment. "How did you get Elliot's phone?"

"He's ill."

Before I can finish, she's talking over me. "Oh my goodness! He's never sick. I'll send someone over right away. You know what? I'll be over myself. Give me fifteen minutes."

Clearly she doesn't think I'm capable of taking care of him. And she doesn't want me alone with him while he's sick.

"We're fine," I say flatly, putting the emphasis on *we*. "I don't need you to come over. I need you to make a grocery order."

There's long beat of silence. "I don't know if that's a good idea."

I do my Minerva laugh, fake and a little mocking. "There are several armed guards watching this place. What do you think a delivery person could do?"

Another long beat of silence. I wonder if she'll come out and just say she doesn't want me alone there with Elliot.

"What does Elliot want?" she asks. "Can you put him on the phone?"

"He's sleeping right now, with a very high fever. He needs his rest, but I could wake him up…"

"No." She says it grudgingly. "I guess if you'd tied him and escaped you wouldn't be calling me to order groceries."

I smile to myself. "No, I wouldn't. Can you help me? Us?"

When she speaks again, some of the hostility has left her tone. "Give me your list and I'll take care of it."

"Thank you." I start to tick off what I need. "Herbal tea, 7UP, crackers, chicken noodle—" I stop, reconsider. "No, wait. Get me a whole chicken, celery, garlic, onions, carrots, and egg noodles. And some good bread."

"Are you making chicken noodle from scratch?"

"Yes." I nod, although she can't see me. I haven't cooked in so long, and I suddenly can't think of anything I want to do more. If I'm going to make some soup, then I'm going to make some *soup*.

"Okay," Anjie says reluctantly. "Anything else?"

"Um, eggs and bacon too." I can make some breakfast as well.

"Is that all?"

"Yes. And thank you again."

Once I've hung up, I head back downstairs and start pulling out the pots, pans, knives, and utensils I'll need. Elliot might not have any food, but he's got a well-stocked kitchen tool wise.

The knock at the door thirty minutes later makes me jump even though I'm expecting it. Although maybe not quite that quickly.

One of the security guards is there, holding four or five grocery bags. "You ordered these?"

"Thank you so much." I'm considerably nicer to him than I was to Anjie as I take the bags. "I've got it from here."

"Is everything in there? The delivery person needs confirmation."

I do a quick visual check. "Yep. It's all there."

Upstairs, I can hear Elliot yelling.

The security guard glances at the noise, then back at me.

"He's sick," I explain.

"That's what Ms. Caprice said. Hope he feels better."

I give the guard a wave in farewell, then set the bags in the kitchen before I head up the stairs. Elliot is still yelling for me.

"I'm coming," I call up.

"What the fuck?" is how he greets me. He's trying to sit up, but he's only gotten halfway. "Who was that?"

"Grocery delivery." I put my hands on my hips as I study him. He looks awful.

"You had groceries delivered?" He tries for "thunderous frown" but only hits "mildly confused."

"I had to. You need food. Real food." I try to push him back down, but he won't budge. "And the guards brought it to me."

"It's still dangerous. You shouldn't have done that."

Scolding Elliot might be my favorite pastime. He's just so deliciously stern. I want to kiss that frown off his face and then make him frown all over again.

"Well, I did it anyway." I give up on trying to get him to lie down. "Trust me, once you taste my chicken noodle soup, you'll thank me."

He flops down on his own. "You're making soup? From scratch?"

I nod.

"I don't need this," he rumbles ungratefully.

"Are you this mean to whoever usually takes care of you when you're sick?"

"Nobody takes care of me when I'm sick." He lies back against the pillows with a long sigh.

"Oh."

His expression goes fierce. "Don't look at me like that. No one takes care of *you* when you're sick."

"You did."

He doesn't say anything, just closes his eyes.

That's my cue to leave him to sleep.

But as I get off the bed, he takes my hand. Not my wrist or my arm, but my hand. And his grip is gentle.

"Please stay." It's not a command. Or even a request. It's a plea.

Can he hear my heart cracking? Because I certainly can.

"Sure." I lie next to him, tucking my knees and arms close to me. I'm on top of the coverlet and he's under it—exactly the inverse of when we first shared a bed. "Do you need anything?"

He shakes his head, his hair scuffing along the pillow. It's a soft, intimate sound. "I already feel better."

Without thinking, I roll over and feel his forehead. "Still too hot. Your fever hasn't gone down at all."

"That wasn't what I meant."

I'm suddenly, achingly aware of how close we are. And how his skin is positively burning up under my palm.

CHAPTER 19

When I wake up, she's still there.

Minerva in her sleep is something else. She curls in on herself like a hedgehog, all prickly on the outside and soft cuteness on the inside. Her mouth is slightly open, and she's making a noise that's not quite a snore but more than simply breathing.

I reach over to touch her cheek, then stop myself. I might be feeling sentimental—and much, much better, thanks to her nursing—but that's a line I shouldn't cross. Angry kisses and orgasms are one thing. Intimacy is another.

I've already crossed too many lines with her. I have to hold some of them.

I run my hands through my hair, which is slightly damp from the shower. I woke up sometime last night, maybe even the morning, feeling better but also gross. The fever broke, but the sweat still clung to me. So I'd showered, cleaned up my beard and brushed my teeth, then collapsed back into bed. The effort wore me out.

Before I did though, I put Minerva under the covers since she looked cold.

I have to go into the office today. I need to question Dev more closely about what he's up to, see what Finn's come up with, and research more of Minerva's legal options. I've got some contacts at the FBI—there might be some way to grant her some kind of immunity if she comes forward.

It's not likely though. All the cases I've read don't end well for the whistle-blowers, especially when it comes to evidence as explosive as this, involving two very secretive government agencies.

"Hey." She stretches and opens her eyes, her shirt pulling across her chest. Her nipples—

I make myself look away.

"Feeling better?" she asks. Before I can stop her, she's got her palm on my forehead. "Oh yeah, the fever's gone."

"I just needed a few hours' sleep."

She laughs. "A few hours? Try a whole day. I roasted an entire chicken and made soup while you were sleeping."

"Really?" I don't remember any of that. "How did you get the groceries?"

"I called Anjie."

I suddenly remember Dev saying that she'd emailed a reporter. She could have done anything while I was asleep. My laptop was sitting out in plain sight.

"Is that all you did?" It comes out angrier than I wanted, but the thought of her sneaking around with my laptop is a burr in my brain.

"Pretty much." She looks innocent. But she's also very good at acting.

"You shouldn't have done that."

She's not fazed. "It'll help you feel better once you eat something decent. Even better than you do now."

I don't feel better. I feel frustrated and surly and amped up. Like I'm a starving bear being teased with food.

Her hand drops. "You don't have to say thank you. My reward is your improved health."

I hate it when she's right. "Thank you. But if anything had happened to you…"

"I know." She blinks. "I was afraid too. But you're well now."

Our gazes lock for a long moment. My skin crackles with the energy between us. She's so close, looking so delicious, so tempting.

I clear my throat, shattering the tension. "I have to go in today."

She ducks her head, nods. "I figured. But you can eat first."

I follow her downstairs. She bustles around the kitchen, heating up the soup, some chicken, and some bread. It all smells amazing.

"You cooked all this?" I ask.

She nods as she sets a bowl and plate in front of me. "I used to like to cook. Before."

I take a sip of the steaming soup, then close my eyes. Goddamn, but that's amazing. "This is the best chicken soup I've ever had."

She smiles and ducks her head. "I'm out of practice." She tucks into her own bowl, and for a few moments we simply share a meal together. I haven't had a home-cooked meal in... forever, and every bite is bliss. She's right—I feel so much better.

"I've been looking at legal remedies for you." I make my tone hopeful although it's unnatural to me.

"Yeah," she says heavily. "I'm guessing there aren't many." She lifts her head. "How did you become a lawyer? And end up at a venture capital firm?"

I don't know that anyone's ever asked me that. People just seem to assume that I was born a lawyer or something.

"My dad." My chest gets tight at the very mention of him.

"Oh. So he was a lawyer too."

I shake my head. "He wasn't anything but a fuckup."

"Really? But you're so..." She gestures at me as if to say *Look at you.* "You're the farthest thing from a fuckup."

I don't let the praise get to me. "Dad never held a steady job. Not once. Every few months he'd come home, say that this time it would be different. That this was his big chance. And then like clockwork, he'd come home talking shit about management, his coworkers, how they fucked him over and he was glad to be rid of that job anyway."

I remember each and every time it happened too. Probably because the script never changed. It was never his fault, always someone else's.

"I'm sorry," she says quietly.

I shrug, short and sharp, because my chest is too tight for anything else. "The worst was the get-rich-quick schemes. He'd lose a job, then take whatever money Mom had managed to save and throw it all away on bullshit. Just utter bullshit. I could see it as a kid even, so that tells you how fucking dumb he was."

All the old bitterness is running through me, acid across my tongue. I don't tell people about this because I know I get too mean. Too nasty.

He's your father. You have to love him. That's what Mom always said.

Well, no, I didn't. Not when he was responsible for all our miseries as a family.

Minerva isn't shocked. Her head is cocked, her expression open. Like this is all interesting instead of appalling. "You hate him."

I open my mouth to protest, but she stops me.

"No, I recognize it. Because you hate me too."

I let my gaze fall to my bowl. "I don't hate you. Not anymore. But I do hate him. I'm not supposed to, but I do."

Her hand steals across the table, finds mine. I don't curl my fingers around hers. I just let her hold on to me.

I don't want her to say that it's okay, that it's understandable, or even worse, that I don't really hate him. Because I really do. And it's an awful feeling.

"So you became a lawyer because you needed order," she finally says. "And because you really like to argue."

"There was so much goddamn chaos." I close my eyes, held against my will by the memories. "Like… like steel wool against my fucking brain, all the time."

Her fingers tighten on mine. "I'm sorry. I know… It's hard to be in a place that makes you fight your own nature."

Meaning that working for Corvus was kind of the same for her.

"What were your parents like?" I'm genuinely curious. "What kind of upbringing produced a Minerva Dyne?"

My path to becoming Elliot Martell is pretty clear. Uptight kid is raised by an out-of-control loser, becomes an even more uptight adult in response. Her path is completely unclear though.

"That's not my name." She says it so simply I almost think I've misunderstood. "It's Emily." Her mouth flattens. "That's who I am. Emily."

I don't dare move, like I've sighted a deer in the woods or something. She didn't realize she'd given me her name before… but she's doing it knowingly now.

This wide fluttering in my chest must be trust. Because nothing else could explain what's happening between us.

"Emily." I test it out, fitting it to the woman before me. Because she's not really Minerva, not anymore. Minerva would never be this soft, this giving. And while I was attracted as all hell to Minerva, it's nothing like the need I feel for her now. "Emily."

She smiles, kind of shy. "Yeah. My parents were… ordinary people. Good people, kind, but I was always hard into these causes. Save the whales, recycle, stop eating meat." She puts a hand over her mouth. "I used to be a vegetarian." She raises a stricken gaze to mine. "But Minerva wouldn't have been one."

I turn my hand over in hers. When my fingers curl closed,

I completely encompass her hand. "You can be one again. I'll order fake chicken noodle soup instead."

She shakes her head, grabs her stomach. For a moment I wonder if she's going to be sick, if I need to grab a trash can. But all she does is push her plate away. "It's okay," she says. "I'm just glad I was able to make something for you."

"I'm glad too," I say.

We share a smile, wry and a little battered. Kind of like us.

When she speaks again, her tone is steady. "So, my parents. They loved me but were baffled by me, I think. They died in my senior year of high school, a car accident. I was already eighteen, so I just… finished on my own. Sold the house on my own, went off to college on my own."

I take our plates since we're both finished. Once they're in the sink, I pull her to her feet and we head back upstairs. I need to get ready, and she… I want her close to me.

"Would they have been proud of you? Your parents?" That's a foreign concept to me. Dad died before I finished college, not that he cared about my education, and Mom was always too tired from cleaning up after him to lavish much praise on us.

Logan was proud when I finished law school. He was there to hug me when I walked across the stage to get my degree.

Her face twists up. "I don't know. Honestly, they would've tried to talk me out of it. And they probably would've succeeded. They had smaller dreams and ideals. Stuff that was closer to home."

I don't know that the mixture of admiration and affection in my chest is pride, exactly. Pride seems simpler than this. And I don't want to say something as silly as "I'm proud of you."

"Emily."

Her head snaps up, and there's a flash of deep pleasure in

her eyes. No one's called her by her real name in forever, and she likes it.

"Elliot." She says it slow and careful, like she's never said it before. And maybe she hasn't. I can't remember.

"I like the way you say my name." It seems to fit me better coming out of her mouth.

"I like the way you say mine."

Everything shifts then, goes crackling and sharp. Like the air is carrying way too much charge, ready to spark against anything it can.

Her eyes are deep, dark, the color of fall leaves. I can't look away. But then there's the sweep of her cheekbones, the curve of her lips, the beat of her pulse in her throat. I want to lick it, press my tongue hard against it.

"Elliot."

When she says my name like that, breathless, needy, I'm a fucking goner. To hell with lines and caution and what we should be doing.

I gather her close and kiss her.

CHAPTER 20

Elliot is never gentle.

I know that by now, but it's coming home in an entirely new way as he's kissing me. The man was on death's door not even a few hours ago, but he's kissing me like…

Well, there's no other way to put it: he's fucking my mouth. All hungry and urgent and demanding.

I wrap the hem of his shirt around my fist and tug upward. If I can't get at his bare skin in the next few seconds, I won't be responsible for what happens.

He stops kissing me long enough to get his shirt off, then dives in for another round. My clit is already throbbing, achy, and he's barely even touched me.

I run my hands over his chest, moaning at the sensation of all that hair. It's just so primitive. Makes me feel wild and free myself.

When I find his nipples, give them a tweak, he rumbles deep in his throat. I have to swallow the sound because he hasn't released my mouth. I run my hands down his pecs, using my nails just a bit. Just to remind him that I can be primal and wild too.

He takes my lower lip between his teeth, bites down softly. Not gently, because there is a difference. And the difference sends tremors of pleasure echoing through my belly, pooling in my pussy.

As if he knows, he finds my sex, presses snug against it. It's good, but I twist up, seeking more.

"I miss your pajamas," he says. "They were so fucking sexy."

"I could tell." I gasp as he rubs me through my panties. He's not even near my clit, but I'm already seeing stars.

"These clothes have to go."

My eyes flutter closed, because *bossy*. Who knew that Elliot Martell ordering me around in that tone was better than any vibrator?

And then he's undressing me. Again, not gently. Some alarm in my brain is telling me to slow down, that he's been sick, but it's like trying to wake up from some deep dream. The alarm is so annoying, so faint, and the dream is so much better.

"Are you okay?" I manage to get out just as he's pulling off the yoga pants.

He frowns. It's a *what the fuck are you on about?* frown. "No," he says bluntly. "You're still wearing your panties. And I have to eat you out."

My mouth falls open. He said it like... like he said *tits* before. So natural, so common, which makes it all the dirtier. Discovering all these new sides of Elliot has been a delight. He just... delights me.

He doesn't seem to notice my shock—he's too intent on tugging my underwear past my ankles. He lets my panties drop to the floor without even a backward look.

Instead, he's staring at me. Like he's going to unlock every bit of me in a few moments. As raw and open as I feel with him, I want to let him. With deliberate motions, he positions me on the pillows, my back propped against them, my chest high and my legs wide.

He leans back on his heels, takes in what he's done. Like if he doesn't get me at the perfect angle for this, it will all be ruined.

Meanwhile, I'm so worked up by his hands on me he could breathe on my pussy and I'd climax.

He nods once, as if satisfied, then leans over…

"Fuck," I hiss out.

His beard is dragging along my inner thighs and it's like too much. My head thrashes on the pillows and my thighs clamp shut.

At least they try to. Elliot grabs my knees, holds me open. Licks my pussy long and slow.

My toes curl and my lungs seize. He doesn't relent. He licks me like he fingered me—trying every kind of stroke, testing every secret, tender spot. Using his lips, his teeth, that way-too-clever tongue. I can't hide from him even if I wanted to.

I take his head, grind myself into his mouth. He makes an eager, encouraging noise that vibrates through me. So I do it again, searching out that friction I'm desperate for.

I'm so close. The orgasm is inside me, trying to claw its way out. Only inches more to go…

Elliot's mouth closes over my clit and he sucks. Hard.

That's all I need to fall over the edge. Elliot doesn't stop though. He keeps it up, pushing me to another peak. And yet another.

When he finally slows down, lets me catch my breath, I'm boneless. Rubbery. He's dissolved me in orgasms.

The gleam in his eye tells me he knows exactly what he did. He cocks one eyebrow. "Speechless, huh?"

Oh, if I could move, I'd toss a pillow at him. Toss a pillow, then snuggle close to him. Let that chest hair scratch against my cheek. Breathe in his scent, savor his heat. Hold him and let him hold me. Savoring each other.

He's on his knees, sitting between my thighs. Beautifully bare chested…

My gaze runs lower. And he's magnificently hard.

This time when I reach for him, he doesn't stop me. Instead, he closes his eyes, sighs. His cheeks are stained dark, but not with fever.

Even through the soft weave of his pajama pants, touching his cock is like gathering sparks. Hot and buzzy in the palm of my hand.

He hooks his thumbs into his waistband and drags his pants off. I catch a glimpse of muscular thighs, hard shins, tight calves, and then he's kneeling again, his thighs spread to offer me his cock.

I wet my lips, move my hand over him. His cock is thick, the veins stark. And his balls are heavy, thick with hair. Again, it's like discovering a secret—tucked into his practical black boxer briefs is this beast. Just like with the chest hair and the dirty talk.

"Do you remember what you said?" His voice is rough, like he had to drag the words out.

"About your hard, thick cock in my mouth?" I look up at him through my lashes. I keep stroking him, tugging hard when I reach the root.

"Yes." The *s* dissolves into a hissed exhale.

I run my tongue along my upper lip, teasing him. "What about it?" Coy, as if my thighs aren't shaking with the urge to taste him.

"You're a monster."

I lower my head. "So sweet," I say. "Just the best compliments."

"A beautiful, maddening monster." He puts a hand to the back of my neck, asking me to go lower. "The sexiest, smartest—"

I close my mouth on his cock, which shuts him right up. I'd smile, but my mouth is too full. He's even thicker, harder like this. The crown nudges the back of my throat.

I run my tongue up and down his length, positioning

myself so he can see everything. I get him nice and wet, cupping the weight of his sac as I attend to every inch of his cock with my mouth.

He runs his fingers through my hair, closing his hand tight. He tips my head back, sets the purple head of his cock at my lips.

There's a question in his expression. *Is this okay?*

I nod. This is all more than okay—this is exactly what I want. Need. He tastes like sweat and musk and hard, grinding sex. He thrusts into my mouth, and with every move, my clit pulses in time.

I clench my thighs together, but it isn't enough. So I reach between my legs with one hand and find my clit.

"Mmmm," I moan around his cock. He thrusts faster, harder. My hand between my legs keeps up with his tempo.

Soon enough, he's coming and I'm coming, all messy and entwined. I release his cock with an audible pop. It gleams with my spit and his come.

We both sort of fall over together, him landing below me on the pillows. Low enough to give my breasts a nuzzle, more like *hello* than *Hello!* Sweet and affectionate. Almost, almost gentle.

I reach over and rub his beard. "This is magical." My voice is slurry with pleasure. And my thighs tingle from the marks his beard left on them. My heart… I don't want to examine the state of my heart.

He reaches up, wipes my lips with his thumb.

"I have to go," he says, "But tonight…" He leans in, kisses me deeply. He must taste himself in my mouth, but it seems to turn him on.

I can still taste hints of me on his lips, and I can confirm: it's hot as fuck.

Don't go, I want to say. *Stay here with me.*

But I know better. And he did promise me tonight.

"I'll be waiting."

I'm deep in a contract—and trying not to get distracted by thoughts of Emily—when a knock comes at my open office door.

My head jerks up. There's Logan, standing in the doorway and holding two brown paper sacks.

"Lunch?" He holds up the bags. "From that burger place over on Alma."

"You brought me food?" Logan can be the typical protective older brother, but he doesn't usually feel he has to feed me.

Logan shrugs. "I thought we could talk too."

Great. I already know what this is going to be about. But he *is* my brother. "Let's eat on the patio."

The day is pleasant, I guess you could call it. Not warm but not chilled. And the breeze is quiet instead of rising up and running through the patio columns.

Logan hands out the food, always the older brother. He knows who gets what, and I simply have to accept what he gives me.

But he also knows my favorites, has since I was born. So I get a roast beef sandwich, piled high with banana peppers, au jus to dip it in, and jalapeño chips along with a Dr. Pepper to wash it all down.

Not exactly a complicated order, but Logan knows it without my even telling him.

"Thanks for this," I say. "I didn't even realize it was lunchtime."

Logan picks up his own sandwich. Pastrami on rye, thickly smeared with Dijon mustard. I'd know that without him telling me too. "I heard from Finn you were sick. You look okay."

"Just a fever. It's gone now." I watch him eat. Logan's always looked more like Dad than I do, with his nose and the way his eyes sit in his face. "Do you remember that one time we were both sick and Dad convinced Mom to go to work anyway? That he'd take care of us?"

Logan snorts. "And the asshole took us to the track. Had some foolproof scheme to bet on the horses."

I shake my head. "It was worse than that. It was a dog racetrack, remember?"

Logan cocks his head. "No, I don't. I could have sworn it was horse racing."

"Dogs. Because he figured fewer people were betting, so he was sure to win."

The whole thing reeked of desperation and sadness. The dogs, the spectators, even the stupid mechanical rabbit.

"You're probably right. I just remember being so hot. Like I'd turned into a furnace."

"He lost the grocery money for the entire month. Luckily, Mom found Hamburger Helper on sale. Remember?"

Logan's expression is grim. "I hate that shit."

Most families get together and remember happy times, laugh together over well-worn stories. Logan and I talk about all the times our old man fucked up.

Logan exhales deeply, rolls out his shoulders. "That's all over now. Dad's dead, and Mom's all set up in her house with her trust. No matter what happens to us, she's taken care of."

It's true. Dad might have failed her, but in the end, Logan and I made sure she was safe. That she wouldn't die penniless.

"How's Callie?" I ask after a few bites.

Logan doesn't smile, but he does start to… *glow*. "Great. The baby's kicking away. Any day now and you'll be an uncle."

I can't help but smile. "And you'll be a dad. Are you ready?"

"Hell no. I'm already terrified. Imagine how much worse it will be when the baby's finally here."

"You'll do great." I'm not just blowing sunshine up his ass —he'll be great. He's already devoted to Callie. He'll be even more devoted to their kid.

"You have to help too, Uncle Elliot."

I'm definitely not ready for that. Uncles are supposed to be fun, supposed to let you do all the things your parents won't. I'm too rigid for that.

"Calling the baby *it* is weird. Could you please find out the sex beforehand?"

"Callie wants to be surprised." Logan sounds like he doesn't though.

"Isn't getting a baby a big enough surprise?" I'd go crazy not knowing. Why would you willfully keep that kind of information under wraps?

"Whatever Callie wants, she can have."

Of course, the guiding principle of Logan's life. Everything for Callie. When she left him, he had nothing left. He just kind of… went hollow. It scared me, seeing my brother like that. And didn't help endear Callie to me.

But it's all fixed now. Logan's forgiven her, and she's forgiven him. I'm… happy for them. Really.

Logan sets down his sandwich. Uh-oh, I know that look.

"You sure you're okay? I know you don't like people in your space."

It's true, but Emily isn't in my space. We're sharing it. And I'd better be careful to not slip up and call her Emily.

"It's fine. We're dealing."

"I'm sure you are—you're good at that," Logan says. "But she seems to get at you. In a way other people don't."

He has no idea. "What do you mean?"

"Like at the partners' meeting. You were practically defending her. I'm just wondering if having her stay with you is messing with your head."

I set my own sandwich aside. I'm done. "I promise you, my head is fine. You're all against her, and I understand why, but she's brought out some incredible information. And completely blown up her whole life to do it."

Logan shifts in his seat, props his elbow against the table. "You just have to take up a struggle, don't you?"

"Struggle? What are you talking about?"

"People say you love to argue—hell, I say it too—but it's more than that for you. You don't argue about stupid shit, like saying the sky is purple just to be a contrarian ass. The argument has to matter to you. The struggle."

It sounds too much like when Emily was talking about the things that mattered to her. Save the whales. Stop the war. Keep on with the struggle.

My chest is tight, my throat clogged. I don't like being so seen, not even by my own brother.

But hell, if we're doing raw confessions here, I might as well go all the way. I clear my throat. "When you fell in love with Callie, how did you… How did you know?"

Logan's very confused. "I just knew. I can't explain it in words. Why, have you met—" His mouth tenses. "Oh fuck. Oh fuck me."

"It's not—"

"It's her." Logan makes it sound like I've caught the plague. "Did you fuck her?"

I tighten up. She's not the plague. "That's none of your business."

"Goddamn it, you did." He pinches the bridge of his nose. "That's why you're defending her."

"I thought I liked the struggle," I say dryly.

"The struggle *and* sex."

"We didn't have sex." And now I'm parsing the meaning of *sex* like a true lawyer.

"But you think you're in love with her."

My heart gets squirrely. I'm not *in love* with her. I like her, sure. I'm worried for her. She… she connects with me in a way no one else ever has.

But it's not love. It can't be. "I never said that."

"Then why did you ask about it?" Logan raises his eyebrows like he's scored a game-winning point. Which might be fair.

"Can we forget about this? I thought we were in the trust tree here." Logan's the only person I know who's fallen crazy head over heels in love with someone. I just wanted to know which symptoms to worry about.

"Always." Logan grins. "But I'm still going to ride your ass." He gets serious again. "Whatever's going on with you and Minerva, I hope you know what you're doing."

I slump in my chair because I'm pretty sure I don't. I don't like this out-of-control feeling, like I have to be with her, see her, hold her. Especially since we have no future as a couple, even if she weren't likely to go to jail.

It isn't love—I don't even know her real last name—but whatever it is, it's got me worried. Not worried enough to stop sleeping with her though, which should terrify me.

Yeah, you could say she's gotten into my head.

"It's complicated," is all I say. When Logan opens his

mouth again, I cut him off. "Remember when you and Callie were having all your issues and I tried to be supportive?"

"That was supportive? Because you kept telling me to divorce her."

"I was worried about you."

Logan reaches over and clasps a hand on my shoulder. "And I'm worried about you. I can't help it."

His hand is heavy on my shoulder, a solid weight that won't budge. It's a hell of a comfort.

"Thanks," I say. "And I know that all this is… not ideal."

Making me chicken soup, taking care of me when I'm sick, cuddling with me: these are not things I do with anyone. It was always going to be a brief interlude even if I wasn't expecting it to be so… nice.

"Yeah. I hate to say it, but there's almost no way she's got a happy ending coming." Logan lifts his hand, sits back.

I make myself sit up, straighten up. Slouching just doesn't feel good after a while. And feeling sorry for myself won't help anything.

"I know there's no happy ending," I say. I make my voice firm, steady, because there's no getting around that truth, no matter how badly I might want to. "And so does she."

CHAPTER 22

Once Elliot is gone, I sleep some more. Sometimes I feel like I could sleep for weeks.

I definitely need it after being sick, then taking care of Elliot. Oh, and the orgasms that wrung me out. When I finally get out of bed, get showered, and head downstairs, it's lunchtime.

I haven't slept in for a very long time. I also haven't taken a day off. Fuchs expected me to be at his beck and call all day, every day, No weekends, no vacations.

I'm going to have to learn how to relax all over again. But first, lunch.

Chicken noodle soup does not appeal. When I look in the fridge, I find several take-out boxes and a note on top: ALL VEGETARIAN.

The handwriting is controlled, precise. And practically screams *Elliot.*

He must have brought these in while I was asleep. I wish he'd woken me up, but he did promise me tonight.

I grab a box and open it. There's mushrooms, squash, kale, and quinoa in a savory-looking sauce. My mouth is already watering.

When I reach up to open the microwave, I see it. And stop dead.

His laptop. Sitting on the coffee table.

Slowly I set the take-out box on the counter, my heart thumping. He had to have left it on purpose. It's out in the open, waiting for me to find it.

The hard drive is next to it.

This is exactly the chance I've been waiting for. So why aren't I breaking land-speed records to open up that computer?

I don't know. My legs feel weighted. My heart too.

If I send off what's on that drive to the press, that's the beginning of the end. I won't be able to stop what happens next.

And what happens next is my going to prison.

I look around the houseboat, at the cozy, snug home Elliot's made here. I want to stay here, to take tiny, tentative steps back into the world, then come back to this. This sense of protection. Belonging.

But it's all an illusion. The protection is paid for and the belonging…

I purse my lips, breathe through my nose to keep from crying. The belonging is only lust. Elliot likes to argue. I like to argue. We sparred together, built up some sexual tension, and then released it.

I don't know if I actually believe that, but I've got to make myself think it in order to psych myself up for what I have to do.

The laptop opens with a soft sigh of the hinges. The home screen immediately pops up, doesn't even ask for a password.

I shake my head. First his phone, now this. Elliot really needs to do something about his computer security. This is just sad.

But it makes it easier for me. In a few moments I've got the drive up and running. I scroll through everything, through the masses of documents and files and memos and programs I stole over the years. I'm trying to find something good to send to the journalist, but it's more like a walk through the past.

There's the first project I worked on at Corvus, the one that caught Arne's eye. It wasn't that complicated—using machine vision and AI to automate monitoring twenty-four-hour camera footage—but I got it done in half the time allotted and better than the initial specs called for. So Arne called me up, asked if I was interested in something different. More challenging.

It was the exact opportunity I'd come for, and I grabbed it with both hands. I kept climbing up the ladder, leaving wreckage in my wake. And on this drive I've cataloged every bit of that wreckage.

I find some things that ought to make the reporter's eyes drop out of his head and should be easy enough to verify if he's got the right contacts. And then I install the secure messaging program on the laptop.

When I enter my info and call up my conversation with the reporter, I see that he's sent me another message: *Still there?*

I could ignore it. I could take the drive and drop it into the canal, get a flight to somewhere else, somewhere far away from here. Fuchs won't forgive and he won't forget, but I could be Emily Dove again for a while. At least until he finds me again. Which could be years.

But that vision doesn't appeal. Not at all. I want the fight. I want to bring Fuchs down or die trying.

I guess the old Emily really is back.

I start to type a message. *Still here. My internet access is limited. But I have some stuff for you.*

Immediately he starts to message me. *Are you a Corvus employee? How did you get the information? Are you still working there?*

I hesitate. Should a reporter be asking all this? He'll need to verify and corroborate everything I send him, but this feels like too much. Or maybe I'm paranoid.

I no longer work there. I haven't exactly turned in my resignation letter, but it's true.

What was your position in the company?

Okay, that's too far. *Do you want to see some of what I have or not?*

There's nothing on the screen for a long time. Long enough to make me think he's gone. And then: *Yes.*

So I send what I pulled aside for me. I don't let myself think or hesitate, just like I walked into Corvus my first day on the job. This was the path I was determined to walk. So I'm going to follow it.

The files upload quickly. Painlessly.

I'll be in touch. And then the journalist is gone.

I methodically remove all traces of the messaging app from Elliot's computer. And then I look up flights to Ecuador, do some searching on the dark web for fake IDs. I also check my email accounts. There's still nothing from my old friends. But of course, Reagan will never be able to answer me, Chad probably doesn't want to, and Deena… Well, we all grow out of that youthful activism stage. Except I got stuck in mine.

I scrub all that from the browser history. Every last trace of me touching Elliot's laptop. If I leave it, he'll figure out what I'm up to.

I'm worried he might stop me if he does. And I'm even more terrified that he won't. If he knows that I'm escaping again and just lets me go…

I shut the laptop with a firm push of my open hand. It's done. There's no going back now.

Not that I ever really had the option.

I practically break the door down when I get home.

If the security detail notices how quickly I'm walking, how I don't even acknowledge them as I hop onto the boat, I don't give a shit. I've got condoms in my bag, and Emily is waiting inside for me.

When I fall into the entryway, she's in the kitchen, watching me wide-eyed. "Is everything okay?"

"Upstairs." I sound like a goddamn Neanderthal, but I can't help it. "Now."

She holds very still for a moment and then she's gone, up the stairs like someone's chasing her.

I grab the box of condoms and let my briefcase fall to the floor. I take off after her, leaving one shoe on the fourth step, the other on the eleventh step. My jacket comes off at the top of the stairs.

She's halfway through getting her own clothes off and is only in a sports bra and yoga pants. When I reach for the buttons of my waistcoat, she snaps out, "No. I'm taking that off you. And all the rest."

She stalks over, and I have to catch my breath at the way her skin plays over the muscles of her stomach, her ribs. She reaches for the bottom button and tugs hard. "These suits are a fucking tease, you know that?"

My suits have been called retro, stuffy, and Atticus Finch-chic, but never a *tease*.

"You do know it," she says. "All this gray tweed"—she flicks a fingernail against the button and my cock twitches —"to cover up what you really are underneath."

"And what's that?" My voice sounds like I dragged it out of the depths of the bay.

"You pretend to be a respectable lawyer." She rises up on her toes, her breasts brushing over my chest. She nips my earlobe and I shudder. "But underneath you're the man who wants to fuck me."

This woman. *This woman.* "Get it off then."

She laughs, wicked, edged, a hint of Minerva creeping back. I like it.

And then she's easing open the bottom button, so slow I know it's deliberate. I have to hold my breath or else my lungs will burn up. Once it's open, she slips her hand into the gap, finding my belly under my shirt. Every muscle from the tops of my thighs to the bottom of my ribs clenches.

She does the rest of the buttons faster, but still slow enough to have me clenching my jaw by the time she gets my waistcoat off. Her hands slide over my shoulders, cupping appreciatively. She makes this hum in her throat that I have to hear again.

I reach for my belt, but she stops me again. "I have this idea. Vision, really."

Vision sounds… intriguing. "Whatever you want."

"That's right." She unbuttons my shirt but leaves it hanging open. Her hands run down my chest—and again there's that hum I love—until she reaches my belt. With a few quick flicks of her fingers, she's got my belt unbuckled and my pants unfastened. She reaches into my boxers and pulls out my cock, giving it a welcoming stroke.

She steps back, sighing appreciatively. "Perfect. Lawyer in the streets"—she caresses my bare chest—"caveman in the sheets."

I want to laugh, but then she starts pulling off her clothes and I'm gone. I'm already pushing her back toward the bed before she's got her panties fully off.

She lies back and I climb up her, taking in the sight of her. "God, I should have gotten you naked the very first time I saw you."

She laughs, then preens for me. "Right in the middle of a meeting about the Ultra acquisition?"

"You made that comment about my contracts." I squeeze her soft thigh, my fingers sinking into her flesh. "It made me so fucking mad."

She stretches luxuriously. "I loved how mad you were. I wanted to keep at you until you blew your top."

Of course she did. She knows exactly how to wind me up. "Every time I saw you after that, you were so dismissive. Like you'd look at me just to look away." I'm breathing hard, my hand sliding up her thigh. Her skin is smoother than silk. "I'd go out of my mind when you did that."

Her smile is satisfied. "I did it on purpose. Because I saw it got under your skin."

"Were we foreplaying all this time?"

"Maybe? I've kind of been out of the relationship loop. I don't know what things are called anymore."

"Who cares what it's called. We can invent our own terms."

She looks very pleased by that. "Does that mean you're going to do to me things that have no name?"

Jesus. I'm going to have to work hard to live up to that. Luckily, she inspires me to new levels of sexual inventions.

"Sure." I lower my head, kiss between her breasts. She took a shower recently, but the natural scent of her skin seeps through the soap. "But first, you had a vision?"

She makes a sweet noise. "I'm naked."

I nod because we've got that part down. So deliciously naked I can't help but run my hand over her torso, squeeze her breast, tease her nipple.

"And you're only half-undressed. Like you see me and you're so wild for me you don't have time to get your clothes off before you fall on me."

That sounds exactly like the state I was in when I came home. Ready to pull her to the floor and bury myself in her. My cock flexes, bumping against her thigh. Her sweet, succulent thigh.

I reach between us, stroking her folds. She's wet, swollen. More than ready.

"Were you fantasizing about this all day?"

She nods. "Among other things." Then, in imitation of me, she reaches down and cups my dick. "Were you?"

"You know I did." I thrust into her hand, slow, deep. Her grip is tight enough to steal my breath.

She runs her hand down her chest, pinches her own nipple. The sight of her pale fingers against the dark nub, the tip peeping out from between them, almost sends me to my knees.

"Let me." I put my hand on her other breast, tease her nipple to a stiff, proud point. She's whimpering by the time I'm done.

"Now." She's not begging, she's demanding.

I remember her fantasy—me so worked up I can't even get my clothes off—so I boost her up onto the dresser. Her legs fall open, her pussy a wet, bright jewel between her legs.

I find the condom I've got in my pants pocket—smart of Emily to insist I leave them on—and roll it down my straining cock.

In the next heartbeat, I'm deep inside her. I take a minute to catch... not my breath. My thoughts. My emotions.

Because it feels so damn good. Not just her pussy, which

is tight and hot, but her thighs hugging my hips, her arms around my neck. All of her, not only the part clenching around my cock.

And then I start to move and everything is obliterated except the heat between us. She meets my demanding thrusts with eager hip lifts, opening to me beyond what I ever could have hoped for.

She slips a hand under my shirt, finding my back. That small point of contact is painfully intimate.

The rest though… the rest is unrestrained. Uncontrolled. Her nails in my back, my teeth on her shoulder.

"I'm so close," she pants.

"Touch yourself."

I lean back, making space so I can watch her. She fingers her clit, stroking the hood, circling the nub. I pull out almost all the way. When she strokes again, I pump into her. And again and again, stroking her from the inside as she strokes herself.

"Elliot," she gets out from between her teeth. Her pussy ripples around my cock as she comes.

I thrust once more, and then my eyes close as I climax. The orgasm rolls through me like an earthquake, shaking my foundations.

She folds forward, slumping against me. We're still connected, my cock soft inside her, her legs hitched up on my hips. Carefully I lower her legs—she's going to get a cramp—then pull myself out of her with a wet smack. Her juices are running down her thighs and mine, and it's hot enough to get me semihard immediately.

"You're still sick," I say as I gather her up in my arms. Her head tucks under my chin perfectly, like she was made to be carried by me. "You need to rest."

"You're still sick too," she retorts. But it's slurry with sleepiness and the remains of her climax.

"Excellent comeback. You work on that all day?"

When I lay her down in the bed, she shifts until she's snuggled deep in the sheets. And then she pulls me down beside her.

A long, happy sigh leaves her once we're entwined together under the covers. She runs a foot along my shin, rubbing my trousers against my skin. The touch makes my chest feel as if it's filled with bubbles. Warm, happy bubbles. Huh. This has never happened to me before.

I like it. I don't want to let go of this sensation. Or her.

"You should change," she says. But she doesn't let me go.

"In a minute."

"In a minute I'll be ready to fuck you again."

"Big words. Think you can live up to them?"

She smiles against my collarbone. "Watch me."

CHAPTER 24

Is there such a thing as too much sex? Elliot and I are doing our best to answer that tonight, and so far what we've come up with is: no, there isn't.

Although breaks are required. We're taking one right now, lying in each other's arms, simply being together. He's surprisingly, wonderfully cuddly.

If I think about it too much, how much I like him, it starts to ache. Because it has to end eventually.

So I don't. I only enjoy the moment for what it is.

Elliot's hard body under mine, a warm, living, full-body pillow. The tender ache between my legs. The way we both smell like sweat and sex.

He inhales deeply, making my head lift along with his chest. "This doesn't have to end."

I can tell he's been thinking about it. Maybe for a while.

So have I though. "My friends haven't contacted me. And when I release that information, there are going to be a lot of powerful people very angry at me. I might even be looking at a treason charge if they're angry enough."

What I mean is *I'm going to get taken down by these massive forces. Give up on me. Get clear, for your own sake.*

"There could be a way." Stubbornness laces the words.

"What, conjugal visits in prison?"

"No. What about… what about a member of Congress? Aren't they supposed to care about this kind of stuff? Provide oversight? One of them could help provide cover for you while you worked out an immunity deal with a lawyer."

He's grabbing at straws. Tiny, microscopic straws, but he's digging hard for them. It's so adorable it hurts.

"Like who?" I'm willing to indulge the fantasy while we're cocooned in his bed like this. This moment is outside reality, so we can dream big.

"I don't know. There has to be someone."

"With the power to go up against the deep state? All on their own?"

"Yes." He's so certain. I want to believe. "We'll contact them, there will be hearings, and you'll be a hero."

"I don't want to be a hero."

He raises his eyebrows. "You spent five years undercover gathering information. Pretending to be someone else entirely. Cutting yourself off from your whole life."

"It wasn't because I have a hero complex." I prop myself up indignantly.

"Then what was it? Why didn't you stop the first month? The first year? Why keep going?"

It's something I've been asking myself the past few days. "I don't know. I guess I was waiting for some moment where I would know it was enough. That there'd be a sign and I'd know it was time to go. But instead, all these awful things just kept piling up on my record. And I kept doing them. I told myself it was Minerva doing them, that since I was going to expose them, it was… acceptable to keep doing them." I chew on my lip. "But that was a lie. It wasn't Minerva's fault. She was fake, an invention. It was all on me no matter who I was pretending to be."

"Why not cut out sooner then?"

I shrug. "It's hard to explain that place. It's completely

sealed off from everything. Nothing comes in, and you can't go out. Soon enough, the unreality of it seems real." I pick at the sheets. "Which isn't an excuse."

"I'm not looking for an excuse. Just an explanation."

I blow out a long breath. I'm not sure I could explain it to myself. "Part of it was that I was supposed to be Minerva. I'd been her for years and she wasn't bothered by any of it. At some point, I wasn't bothered that much either. I was numb."

He watches me, no judgment but no acceptance in his gaze either. He's simply listening.

"The other thing is, I know Arne is awful, but he was my entire world, day in and day out. Pleasing him… It sounds sick, but eventually I craved his approval. I wasn't getting any kind of comfort or even human contact anywhere else. So I lapped up what I got from him."

Elliot still says nothing. I can't tell if he's appalled or processing that or what.

"But no excuses. Like I said."

Finally he moves, shifting so that he's closer to me. "I just wanted to know." He doesn't say that it wasn't my fault, that he understands, or anything else. I'm immensely grateful because all that would have felt patronizing. He's always met me as an equal, even when he hated me.

I love that he's still doing it now.

"Let's not talk about him," I say. "Let's talk about you. What would you be doing if your brother hadn't struck it rich? If you had to work as an ordinary lawyer?"

Not that he could be ordinary ever.

He puts a hand to his forehead, rubs. Like he's thinking so hard about that he needs the extra push. "I really liked my legal history classes. Laying out the path of how we got from there to here, seeing how the pieces come together."

"What would you have done with that?"

"Maybe been a professor."

Oh yes, I could see Professor Martell in his three-piece

gray tweed suit, sternly lecturing young, impressionable law students about some fine point of the legal system. He'd command his classroom.

"But then Logan got rich and needed a lawyer." The story of the rise of Bastard Capital is a legend in the tech world. Five guys in a garage, working on a stock-price prediction program. It works so well they become overnight billionaires. And then, in a shocking twist, they delete the program and start a venture capital firm.

Elliot wasn't one of those five guys. He came in the day after, to help them work out all the legal issues. But they made him a full partner and gave him an equal share of their riches.

It's the kind of generous loyalty that shouldn't exist. I certainly haven't seen or experienced it.

"I was doing contract and business law before that," he says. "Legal history isn't in high demand in the corporate world."

"That's too bad." I know all about dreams deferred.

"What about you? If someone had managed to talk you out of this"—he clearly thinks he could have if he'd known me then—"what would you be doing?"

"I have no idea. No, really. Back then I hadn't even circled around what I wanted to do for a career, much less settled on it. There was something I loved about everything I studied—history, literature, sociology, even biology. There was too much to learn in all of it to settle on just one thing."

He cocks his head. "But you're so focused."

"Now I am. Working at Corvus will focus you like a laser." I shrug. "I suppose it doesn't matter now what I wanted to be then."

"It does." His voice is softly reassuring. "We both could have had entirely different lives if not for the sharp turns events took."

Lives that might have allowed us to be together, like normal people. "A fantasy life."

He nods. I suppose the magic of this night, warm and huddled with each other under the covers, is making him imagine the impossible.

I shift, settle closer to him. I want to play along. "Where would we have met, in this fantasy time line?"

"When I represented you pro bono for chaining yourself to a tree. Or a whale."

I duck my head, snicker into his throat. Because that would have been likely back then. Maybe not being handcuffed to a whale though.

"The suit would have got me," I say. "I'd have seen you somewhere in the City and had to find you. That suit would be my homing beacon."

I'd be walking somewhere, maybe in SoMa, and my head would be down to protect my neck from the wind. But there'd be a flash of gray, a beard, a stern mouth under that beard, and I'd be hooked. Kind of like I am now.

"Where would we go for our first date?" he asks, assuming that this mythical suit snaring would happen.

I have to think about it a minute. "Here. We'd come here and fuck like rabbits. And then you'd wake up early to get to your corporate job, and I'd sneer at you for being a square, but secretly I'd miss you all day."

He smiles like he loves that idea. "For our second date, I'd take you to Pacifica. There's this restaurant right on the beach that I always wanted to go to. It looks almost like a lighthouse, with massive curving windows bowing out."

"Why haven't you gone?" When I was Minerva, I couldn't simply duck into any place that interested me, but he's Elliot Martell. He can do whatever he wants.

"I was never with someone when I passed it. It's the kind of place that requires good company. Special company."

And he'd take me there on the second date. "Our third date would be… a movie."

"A movie?"

"Yeah." I don't mention that I haven't been to the movies in forever. I don't want to ruin the fantasy. "Get popcorn, soda, and the big candy boxes."

"What movie?" He's still not convinced.

"You could pick. Something artsy or depressing at the Embarcadero theater."

That gets a small quirk of his mouth. He's getting sold on the idea.

"After the third date," he says decisively, "we won't go on any more. We'll just be together. And do things together. You'll move in about a month later, although I'll ask you to after the second date."

Wow. I know it's a fantasy, but the picture makes my throat clog. It sounds like… like falling in love. "I have a lease. I can't just break it."

He makes a noise that says he can do whatever he wants. "When will we get married?"

Marriage. The word catches me up short, seals the breath in my lungs. It's not something I've thought about, at least not seriously. I was too young before I started at Corvus, and then once I was in, relationships weren't even on my radar.

Marriage. It's what you do when you fall in love. I know that much. Maybe…

I close my eyes. This is only a fantasy, but my reaction to that word is way too real.

"If you don't believe in it," he says softly, "we can live in sin. I'm completely happy with that."

That's also something you do when you fall in love; adjust your expectations to meet the other person's.

I'm not ready to answer the marriage question, not even in a made-up scenario. "What about kids?" I ask instead, which might be an even bigger minefield.

He shifts, his expression clouding. "My dad wasn't a great example. Logan's wife is going to have a baby any day now, and he's really excited and he'll be a great dad… but I'd be worried. Hell, I'm only the uncle and I'm worried."

It's so sweet it makes my teeth hurt. Along with my heart.

"Uncles should be worried," I say. "It's a big deal." He's going to be the most concerned uncle ever. That's one lucky kid.

"One," he says decisively. "One kid. And they'll have cousins so they won't be alone."

I can imagine a darling little girl or boy with Elliot's seriousness and his range of frowns, each of them cuter than the next.

My heart unclenches, opens. Yes, I could want that. If we weren't imagining things that could never happen.

"Where would we live," I ask, "us two married people and our one kid?"

"Where did you grow up?"

"San Diego. Well, a suburb of there."

"Some place close to the beach then?"

I shake my head. I'm not that attached to the old neighborhood. "Where did you grow up?"

"Suburb of LA."

Smog and freeways. My mouth curls at the thought. "What about the mountains?"

Somewhere fresh and clean and cold and far away from anything we ever knew.

"I like that idea," he says. "Our kid would run around outside, collect pine cones, have squirrels for friends."

"We'd stay in the same house. We'd find the perfect place and just plant ourselves there." I run my hand over his hair. "No chaos."

"A little chaos is okay."

"Just a smidge? For seasoning?"

"Yeah." His voice is thick with resignation. Like we've come to the end of this fantasy.

I suppose we have, coming to the house in the mountains, happily married with an adorable kid. And a smidge of chaos.

He lifts up on one elbow, his eyes dark. Hungry.

Suddenly we're both back in the very real present and the very real thing we have between us: limitless desire.

"I'm ready," I say to let him know he doesn't have to hold back. Because there's something urgent, fast, lurking in his gaze.

He spins me around so that I'm on my hands and knees and he's behind me, hard, massive. There's a pause—the condom—and then his hands dig into my hips. Deep.

At his first thrust, I understand why he's holding so tightly—because he's fucking me so hard I could slip out of his control. I push back, meeting his need, bracing myself against the mattress.

My orgasm comes on stuttering and quick, waves cresting one right after the other inside me. He pumps harder, faster, grunting with every thrust.

And then he slows, stiffens, coming with a long sigh. Like he's finally found what he was so urgently seeking.

We fall down together, him being considerate enough not to land on me. Not that I'd mind. And then we take another rest.

We don't talk about our fantasies anymore.

This is what we have now, and it has to be enough. Because we're not getting anything else.

CHAPTER 25

My phone rings at what-the-fuck thirty in the morning, jolting me out of a sound sleep. I'm going to ignore it since Emily is pressed close to me, warm and soft. I sigh, tuck my arm into her waist. Oh, and she's still naked.

I managed to lose my shirt at some point last night, but my pants are still on. Barely. My dick is hanging out of my boxers, and I'm already half-hard.

Maybe I can wake Emily up with some kisses. And oral sex.

The phone rings again.

"You should get that," Emily mumbles.

"No." I put my lips to the frontier between her ribs and stomach, reach out my tongue to taste her skin.

"It could be important." She makes an encouraging noise anyway. "Like the baby's here."

I immediately sit up. "Shit. I forgot."

But when I grab the phone, the screen says it's Finn.

"Shouldn't you be asleep like a normal human?" I snap as a greeting.

"Uh, no." Finn actually sounds put out. "I've been working on your shit, so I haven't been keeping track of the time."

"Sorry." I sit on the edge of the bed, then quickly tuck my cock away. "What's happened?"

"I got her. Got everything."

It takes me a moment, but then I make the connection. "You found her."

"Get down here to the secure facility and I'll show you."

I want to look over my shoulder at Emily—I can feel her stare boring into my back—but I resist. She knows what we're talking about; she has to. I'm not going to glance guiltily at her. We had a right to search out her real identity.

I clear my throat. "Be there in a few."

"Sweet. See you then."

I put the phone down but don't look at her. I can feel her attention on my back, like a living weight. "You're coming too."

I don't know why I've just decided that. Maybe... maybe because it's past time for us to be working separately, closed off from each other. If we're going to find a way forward—*all* of us, including her—she has to be included fully.

Emily doesn't say anything, just watches me as I call the head of the security detail, telling him where we're going. And she keeps watching me as I change clothes.

Finally, once I'm dressed and ready, she speaks. "I don't think I should go."

"Why not? You must be sick of this place. And we'll go straight from the car to our building. The guards will be there the entire time."

I suppose Fuchs might try to stage an accident on the freeway, but I'm willing to risk it.

"That was Finn," she says. It's not a question, so I don't respond. "He's been going through my drive."

I find some of her clothes in a shopping bag—she could have put them in the drawers, I wouldn't have minded—and toss them at her. "Yes. But you knew that. You sent him all that information on the panopticon and the back door to Corvus, remember?"

"I sent it to Ramona." A shiver goes through her. "Arne was so furious when they released that virus. There was nothing to salvage from the entire project."

"Wasn't that the point? Isn't that the point of everything you were doing, to leave nothing left to salvage for Corvus?"

She hugs the clothes to her chest. "Yes." Her chin lifts. "Yes. I'll be ready in a minute."

We're at the secure facility owned by Bastard Capital in less than twenty minutes. It's mostly an open room with workstations throughout it. There're a few private offices, but Finn never uses them. Tonight he's at one of the workstations, Ramona at the one next to him.

"Emily Dove," Finn shouts across the room when we enter. I don't think he's seen that she's by my side.

Emily goes stiff. Ramona sees her, and she goes stiff too.

"That's my name," Emily says slowly. "You weren't just going through the hard drive."

Ramona says nothing, but all the blood drains from her face. It's like watching her turn to marble.

I had no idea she was here, but I should have guessed. Fuck, this just went from awkward to painful.

Finn is on his feet, his fist planted on the desk. "What the fuck, man?" He gestures at Emily. "You cannot bring Minerva Dyne into this place."

"This is about her." I take her arm, lead her forward. "So she should be here." Emily doesn't come with me easily, but she doesn't fight.

"It's about her in the sense that she's the one responsible for all this shit." Ramona's voice is as steely as her expression.

I bring us a few feet away from Ramona and Finn, keeping the desk between us.

"You saw what I brought out on that drive. What I sent to you a few weeks ago too. You think I'm lying?" Emily's demeanor is cool, but her fingers are rubbing against her thigh.

I want to take her hand, but that would be too much.

"Great, you have evidence of what a terrible company Corvus is. But you helped do all those things."

"Which is how I was able to get all that evidence out. Only someone within the company, someone very high up, could have access to that." Her voice hitches. "I know what I did there."

"What, you're going to say sorry and that will make it all better?" Ramona sneers.

"No." Emily is getting calmer, steadier. Stonier. "I won't apologize."

Ramona's mouth falls open. "You put my brother in jail."

Shit. My entire body goes tense. This was a bad idea. I don't know if I should hustle Emily out of here or not.

"I did." Her expression is a mask, but her pulse pounds at the base of her throat where only I can see. "Along with several hundred people at Corvus working on that project, with the help of a development company and the upper levels of the police department. I put your brother in jail. Along with over a thousand other people."

Ramona's mouth quivers, like she wasn't expecting that. "But you're the one in front of me now."

"Yes. And I won't shy away from your anger. But it took an entire system to put your brother away—attacking one person isn't going to change any of it."

"It would make me feel better. A lot better."

I shift onto the balls of my feet, ready to come between them. Because Finn doesn't look at all inclined to stop Ramona if she does leap over the table.

Emily folds her hands, accepts Ramona's words. "I had my mission. I've done what I can."

"Mission?" That catches Finn's interest. "What mission?"

Emily's attention swings toward him. "I went undercover

at Corvus five years ago, intending to gather evidence to expose their crimes."

It sounds so simple when she puts it like that, when it was anything but.

Finn whistles. "That explains why it was so hard to find you. I thought maybe you were just covering up a criminal record or something with the fake name. I had to send someone to a library to look at some microfiche. *Microfiche.*" He holds up a photocopy. "You won an essay contest freshman year. They put your picture in the local paper. You managed to wipe it from the newspaper's website, but you couldn't get the physical copies."

He sets it on the desk. *North Park News* is the paper, and there's a younger, eager version of Emily staring back from a grainy photo. I never would have guessed she and Minerva were the same person.

North Park is in San Diego. The dates in the newspaper match up with the timeline she's told me already.

"Parents died when you were in high school—I found the obituary," Finn says. "You went to Berkeley, dropped out early. You or someone else managed to wipe most of your records from the school computers, but I found an email chain between you and one of your professors on a siloed backup drive."

Emily isn't looking at him as he recites all this, but a faint smile plays at her mouth. Like he's figured out a murder mystery before he's reached the end and she's impressed by his powers of deduction.

"You were known for your commitment to various causes. And then one day you disappeared."

Her gaze flicks up. "You didn't find that on any computer."

"No." Ramona cuts in then. "We found Deena Hastrom."

Emily's mouth opens into a perfect O. And then she's

sagging, slumping, and I pull a chair under her before she falls down.

"Deena..." Her eyes are dull with betrayal. "She was supposed to email me. She was my contact, the only one I could count on. And she talked to you?"

Suddenly the entire thing hits me in a rush. All at once. "It's all true."

"You think I lied?" Her voice rises fast, high.

"No, I... It's just that seeing it all together, it's a lot."

"Right." She turns away. "Now that you have testimony from your friend, you believe."

That's not it, but I'm not going to argue here.

"She erased her identity and went to Corvus intending to expose them," I explain.

"For five years?" Finn's eyebrows jerk up.

"Things got away from me," Emily mutters.

Ramona sighs, props a hip against the desk. "Deena didn't say what you were doing at Corvus. Only that you'd disappeared and she didn't know where to find you."

"She was out too," Emily says. "Chad got married, Reagan died, and Deena... quit." She puts a hand to her face. "I really was all alone."

I grab the arm of her chair and squeeze since I can't hold her. "You're not alone." I glare at Finn. "We'll help you."

Ramona looks very, very displeased. Finn looks torn.

"We all want to bring this information out," I say, holding their gazes. "And to bring Fuchs down."

Ramona is the first to look away, chewing her lip as she does. Finn drapes his arm over her shoulder, pulling her in close.

"It'll be okay," he says to her. To me he says, "Should we talk to Callie about this? Get her to publish it?"

Emily's hand falls from her face. "No. You've done enough."

She won't look at me.

"We can help." I keep my tone quiet even as I put some urgency in it. "It doesn't have to be you on your own."

She doesn't say anything. Somehow she's drawn herself away from us. Back into Minerva, the woman who stands alone.

Ramona clears her throat. Does it again. "Think about it. They have the resources."

It's an olive branch of sorts.

Emily looks at her with a clear, steady gaze. But still wary. "I will."

I'll have to work on her more when we get home. Convince her to let us take over, that she doesn't have to go to prison. She's got options, and we can offer her all of them.

My intentions are partly selfish too. I'm not ready to let go of her.

"We should go," I say. "Thanks for finding this."

Finn nods. Ramona crosses her arms.

Then Finn's phone and mine blow up at the same time, pinging us both with a message. We check the screens at the same time.

"Dev," I say.

"What does he want a meeting tomorrow morning for?" Finn says.

"This morning actually," Ramona says, pointing at the clock.

I sigh. There's only a few hours until Dev wants all the partners to meet. "We can talk about Emily's situation then too."

I look at her, daring her to protest.

"You call her Emily?" Finn asks. He's got one eyebrow raised.

Emily rises, turns for the door. "You can all keep calling me Minerva. I know you'll be more comfortable that way."

Finn and I share a look.

"See you in a bit," I say, then go after Emily.

CHAPTER 26

This isn't the first time I've been in Bastard Capital. None of them probably remember, but three years ago I was here offering a buyout for one of their start-ups. That was before Arne and the Bastards declared war on each other, and it was an insubstantial meeting so they could hand over contracts or something. I don't remember the name of the company now—they turned out to not be worth it, and Arne liquidated them a few months after they came to Corvus—but I remember meeting Mark, talking with him for a few moments.

I didn't see Elliot. I would have remembered that.

He's sitting next to me in the conference room. We haven't talked about what Finn found or Elliot's offer to help me.

I'm too raw to discuss any of it. Deena spoke with them but not to me. I can't get over it.

And I'm pissed. She could have sent me… something. We planned this together. I lost my entire life to this—and she can't even email me. But she can talk to the Bastards.

I almost wish I didn't know that. Then I could pretend she just hadn't gotten my email, didn't know that I'd finally gotten out.

I also can't get over that Elliot had Finn searching out my real identity. Logically, I should have expected it, but in my heart… My heart wanted him to believe me.

But I don't deserve his trust. Not after everything I've done. And right now my instinct is to refuse his help. To keep going alone.

Anjie sets a cup in front of me. It smells like coffee, which I desperately need. I'm running on two hours sleep, max.

I don't reach for it.

Elliot drags it toward me, and the noise grates against my ears. Heck, his entire presence next to me feels like an abrasion.

"You need it." The gentleness of his tone… it makes me grit my teeth.

He's also right, which I really hate. I don't want to fall asleep in this meeting. So I take a sip.

It's so delicious it makes me angry. I wanted to hate it.

Ramona comes in with Finn then, and I go rigid.

Learning that Elliot has been investigating me hurt. Facing down Ramona was pure agony.

I didn't know Ray was her brother when I had him framed for robbery. Somehow that makes it worse. Because he was completely faceless, nameless to me, just a homeless man I was going to test our system on.

He had a family. I ruined his life and theirs when I did that.

Putting a face to what I've done… I breathe through my nose, deep and slow. Forcing the air in and out.

I hardly knew who Ramona was when I sent her that information from inside Corvus. All I knew was that someone had broken into Corvus to access the panopticon files and they were trying to break the encryption. So I sent them what they needed. I had no idea who was on the receiving end.

That was when I decided to break out of my mask.

Someone on the outside was trying to help. I wasn't alone. That was my breaking point.

Joke's on me because these people on the outside that I thought were helping have every reason to hate me. And without my armor of being Minerva—cold, uncaring—I'm too raw to be near them. To see what I've done to them.

"More." Elliot points to the cup. "Before it gets cold."

I take a sip, then keep my eyes on the cup as everyone else files in. If they're shocked to see me here, no one says anything. Perhaps Finn already warned them.

Dev is the last one to come in. If he's aware of how the attention in the room shifts to him when he does, he doesn't show it.

He sits down, steeples his hands. Doesn't say hello or call the meeting to order or anything. "I've bought a controlling share of Corvus."

There's a moment of quiet shock, almost denial. *Did he say what we thought he did?* It's followed by a wave of *Holy fuck, he did.*

"In the next few days," Dev says, "I'll have the board vote to oust Fuchs."

Corvus is publicly held, so a takeover has always been theoretically possible. But the company is so entwined with Fuchs and the myth of him—hell, the company *is* the myth of Arne—that it never seemed possible.

My first instinct is to deny that the board will do it. Fuchs has dirt on all of them, some pretty unspeakable stuff in some cases. Like underage girls and bestiality kind of stuff. Things that made my stomach turn to hear about but that Minerva didn't bat an eyelash at.

Dev seems too assured to let a little thing like the board members' scandals slip past him. I wonder what he's found on them, if he's going to use it to twist their arms. Or maybe the promise of freedom from Arne was enough for most of them.

"Holy fuck." That's from Mark. The rest of them are too stunned to speak. "And you were going to tell us about this when? Because this isn't some spur-of-the-moment whim. You had to have been working on this for months. And all behind our backs."

"Not behind your backs." Dev raises a finger. "In secret. Otherwise, it never would have worked."

"You don't trust us." Logan looks very white. Very still.

The shock has coalesced into something colder, harder. Resentful.

I'm trying not to notice Elliot's reaction, but I can't help it. His expression is stricken. Betrayed. "We're supposed to all be in this together. All of it."

Dev's getting annoyed. Or frustrated. I can't tell the difference. "You wanted Fuchs gone. And soon he will be. We'll have control of all of Corvus's assets."

"To do what with?" I ask.

They might be pissed at Dev, but when I speak, they all suddenly remember they hate me. Every face that turns toward me is hard. Except for Elliot's.

"I'd be a fool to tell you," Dev says. "But that hard drive is now our property."

I snort. "You've treated it like yours from the very beginning." If Dev thinks I'll be intimidated by him, he's very wrong. I came up under a harder, scarier man than he'll ever be.

"It had to be contained." He says it as if I'm an idiot or a child. "Release of that information could have jeopardized the takeover."

I suck in a breath. What arrogance. From all of them, Fuchs included. They made their plans, and the mere mortals simply had to get out of the way. God forbid my escape from five years of captivity interfere with his business plans.

"Yeah, that information?" I toss out with careless glee. "I already released it. To a reporter."

"What?" The shock on Dev's face is a pure delight. *Gotcha.* "To who?"

Next to me, Elliot shifts. "Fuck," he mutters under his breath.

I ignore him. "That information is mine. All of it. I spent five years under that psycho, doing terrible things, to get it. I'll give it to whoever I please."

My righteous indignation doesn't even dent Dev's composure. "We know *all* about the terrible things you did."

Right. I want to wrap my arms around myself or reach for Elliot's hand, grab some small bit of comfort and never let go. But that would show weakness. So I don't.

Dev sets his jaw when I don't respond. "We'll have to move quickly then. Before this story breaks."

They all nod, even Elliot.

"I'll start bringing in whatever board members I can," Mark says. "And I'll get Paul on the phone. He probably went to kindergarten or something with some of them."

"I assume you already have a legal team?" Elliot asks Dev.

"Yes, but I need you to take charge of them now."

Elliot nods.

Suddenly the moment where they were all angry at Dev is gone, as if it never happened. They're all united, all committed to making Dev's plan work. To beat the countdown that I started.

Fine. I'm fine with that. I knew none of them were on my side, that I only had myself in all this. I've survived this long on my own, and I'll keep on surviving, without them.

Finn looks to Logan. "We can tackle the other parts of the handover," he says.

Logan nods. "And I'll talk to Callie and Anjie about the media stuff, what we want to release when." His attention swings to me. "When's this story coming out?"

"I... I don't know." God, I wish I had a better, snappier answer. One that would knock them on their asses again.

They all look at Elliot. He shrugs even though his face is dark. "It's my fault. I left her with my laptop and the hard drive. I assumed because you were monitoring the emails she set up…"

My skin goes cold as my stomach knots hard. "Finn hacked those emails," I say flatly. I'd suspected that, but to hear it said out loud… "Looks like I managed to outsmart him though."

Elliot is sitting less than a foot from me, but I've never felt so far from him. Not even when we hated each other.

Finn clears his throat. "She is who she says though. Well, I mean she's not. She's telling the truth. She made up Minerva Dyne and spent all that time at Corvus collecting evidence."

I'd appreciate the show of support more if they weren't all furious that I've finally done the right thing after all this time and released some of what I'd gathered. Or if Elliot—

My lungs hitch. I'd thought he might have begun to at least trust me some, if not have real feelings for me. But everything that's been revealed last night and this morning proves it's all a lie.

"I didn't do it for any of you," I say. "I don't owe you anything."

I say it to all of them, but I really mean it to hit Elliot. It's not true—I owe him my life, among other things—but I want him to hurt as bad as I do.

I've been betrayed over and over again, just in the past few days, and they all hurt. I won't let myself crack because of it, but that won't stop the pain. Elliot turning on me is the worst though. Probably because I was starting to care about him the most.

If my words do hurt him, he doesn't react. His mouth flattens, but it's into his usual frown. His *you're wasting my time* frown.

"What's done is done," Dev says.

That's true. Whatever Elliot and I had feels very done right now.

"But we need to get to work on this," Dev finishes.

With that, they all rise. No one looks at me or says good-bye. I've become invisible, unnecessary. Irrelevant.

As he's walking to the door without even a backward glance, Elliot stops as if he's forgotten something. "Anjie. Arrange for security to take her home." He gestures toward me, then leaves without meeting my eyes.

Dev has really fucked things up.

Mr. Mysterious just had to throw that bomb into the middle of everything, sending us all running to secure this thing. It's a good plan, taking over Corvus and forcing Fuchs out, but he might have said something, anything, while he was doing it.

I've been going back and forth with the legal team for several hours now. They're all good, top-notch even, but there's a million and a half details to be ironed out, and they're not happy about the new sped-up schedule they're on.

Neither am I, but too bad.

My mood isn't helped by the fact that I can't stop thinking about Minerva. I've been slipping up and calling her that again, but that performance in the meeting was pure Minerva. Smuggling information out to a reporter right under my nose? Also pure Minerva.

I'm such a fucking sap. I'd left the hard drive because it was hers and the laptop because I thought she was bored. I knew what she could get up to with a computer, and I still left it with her.

Because I trusted her. I trusted her story that she was

waiting for her friends, trusted that she'd tell me if she'd done anything like that.

But she's been playing her own game all this time. If Finn's story about finding this Deena didn't match up with what Minerva had said about her, I'd suspect her of lying about these friends of hers all along. She wasn't though. She told me the truth, I offered her my help… and she went her own way in the end.

That's what hurts the most.

Anjie pops her head into my office. "You need anything?"

I shake my head. "Just more time. And a way to make the legal system move faster than a snail's pace."

"Sorry, I'm all out of spare time." Her mouth purses. "Minerva got home okay."

Right. I should have asked about that. "Thanks. Look, I know you didn't want to have to interact with her, and I made you. And I'm sorry."

She shrugs, very elegantly. "It was fine. I might have been too rough on her at first."

I might have been too. But now that it's all come to this, was I really?

I close my eyes because I can't take any more questions without answers right now. I force my mind to clear.

I open my eyes, focus on Anjie. "Yeah, I… She didn't really say anything, but I got the impression it didn't go well. None of her interactions here seem to."

Which was the understatement of the fucking year.

"She really was working against Fuchs all this time?"

I nod. "Left behind her friends, her entire life, and became Minerva." She stayed true to her mission through the very end. I have to give her that.

"Emily Dove." Anjie tests the name. "Much softer than I would have expected."

My jaw clenches because I don't need reminding. All of

Emily turned out to be much softer than I would have expected.

"I gave her a burner phone," Anjie says. "In case we need to contact her. She can't call out on it."

Anjie holds out a slip of paper with a number on it.

I take it from her with heavy fingers. "She's not a prisoner." And yet... we took her hard drive. Kept her without internet access. And now we've given her a phone that can't call out. Surrounded her with armed guards.

Anjie says nothing.

"I did what I thought was best," I say. "The situation was unprecedented. There was no right way to proceed."

"I think she might have been trying her best too," Anjie says.

Ah fuck, why didn't she just take a dagger to my conscience instead of saying that?

Minerva did all this alone. Who am I to come along at the end of five years and demand that she trust me, that she give everything over to me? Yes, I feel...

How do I feel about her? I can't put a name to it. It's intense, dark and bright all at once, the joy I had with her tightly bound to the betrayal I felt in that meeting this morning. It's the highest highs and the lowest lows, and they all have her name on them.

I look at the slip of paper in my hands. "I'll call her later," I say. "To see how she's doing."

Anjie nods, pleased, then leaves me to my work. The never-ending work of tying up Dev's scheme into a neat bow. Or noose, considering that we're going to take down Fuchs.

Which just might provide Emily with a path to freedom. The government is still going to be pissed at her for leaking the stuff she has, but if Fuchs is tossed out and in disgrace, they might be less likely to prosecute.

It's a faint hope, but I hold on to it as I keep working.

An hour later, my phone rings. The screen says that the caller ID is blocked. Normally I'd send it straight to voice mail, but some sixth sense has me picking up.

My pounding pulse tells me it's Emily. Maybe she wants to talk, to work through some of the shit storm that's hit us in the past few hours. I don't have time to deal with it, but knowing that she wants to…

"Elliot here."

"I have to make this quick." It's the FBI agent I know, the one I contacted asking about Emily's situation. My heart dips when I realize it's not Emily. "Your girl passed some stuff to a reporter, but he burned her."

"What?" I rise half out of my chair.

"I'm not sure which agency—NSA or CIA—but he asked somebody there about the documents she'd given him, wanted to verify them. But the idiot let slip enough for them to figure out who she was. They're sending a team to arrest her right now."

Everything around me has gone to white noise. My desk, the furniture, my laptop are all fuzzy, indistinct. The only tangible thing is that she's in danger.

"They know where she is?" I ask. If the team is going to her apartment, we have some time.

"Yeah. I don't know how, but they know she's staying with you. You've got maybe twenty minutes before they're breaking down your door. Figured I'd give you a heads-up so you can start working on her bail. If they grant it."

"Thanks." But I'm feeling anything but thankful.

The government is coming after her, just like she feared. No one will ever see what she's risked so much to bring out.

But the thing that turns me to ice, makes my heart stop, is the very real idea of never seeing her again. Of Emily in a true prison, locked away from everything. From me. Of how dark both our worlds would be.

I can't let that happen. Can't let her go.

I run for the door, dialing the number of the burner Anjie arranged for her. If they're already there, she has no way to let me know. And the security detail isn't going to hold off an FBI team.

The phone gives me a busy signal. What the fuck?

I try again. Another busy signal.

The interns are staring as I tear through the offices. Finn passes me, reaching out to grab me.

"What's—"

I dodge him. "No. No time."

I'm speeding out the front door as I dial the head of the security detail. "There's a team of federal agents coming your way," I say the second he picks up. "Delay them until I can get there."

"We can't—"

"I know what you can't do." He doesn't need to waste time on the legal bullshit. "Just… just give me a chance to get to her first."

I open my car door, toss the phone onto the passenger seat without even hanging up. And then I'm off to try to save her any way I can.

I have a laptop, my hard drive, and a cell phone. Everything I need to stay connected in the modern world.

But there's no one out there to reach out to. I already know Deena's not coming, I still haven't heard back from the reporter, and Elliot...

He's not going to call.

I've had a lot of time to process what's happened. Of how we came at cross-purposes to everything. How I couldn't trust him, not with everything, and he did the same to me.

And how he helped me when he didn't have to. And I did the same for him.

Maybe there are some knots that can never be untied. You can only work around them, figure out how to move forward with whatever is tied to you.

If I could call him, I'd tell Elliot that. Not that I'm sorry I didn't tell him about the reporter—I'm not—but that I wish there was a way I had been able to. And that there was a way for him to tell me that he was investigating me, monitoring my email. We couldn't have stopped events, but maybe going forward, we can find a way around this knot even if we can't escape this baggage. Maybe it just means we are, really, tied together.

But all I can do is stare at the phone and think. And obsessively check the secure messaging app. The reporter seems to have disappeared. It shouldn't take him this long to verify what I sent.

Unless his publisher is too scared. Or decided the story wasn't worth pissing off the intelligence establishment. Or just ghosted me for no reason at all.

I also refresh all the tech-news sites, watching for a story on the takeover of Corvus. If Dev really does have everything in place, he'll have to move quickly. It's like grabbing a cobra by the tail—if you hesitate, the cobra will strike. You have to snatch quick and clean. And the cobra fights anyway.

Fuchs is going to fight. I'm not entirely sure how—I know how he operates with the full might of Corvus behind him, but alone and cornered? That's going to be an entirely different Arne Fuchs then.

I suppose I could have helped them with the last push of the takeover. No one knows Arne better than I do. But of course they wouldn't trust me with that. And I don't know that I wanted to be asked. I meant it when I said I didn't do all this for them.

I'm still independent. And I still like it that way.

I'm checking another website, this one filled with rumors about impending company demises and takeovers and general incompetence, when the phone rings.

I blink at it. It could be Elliot—there's no caller ID, not that I know his number anyway.

My fingers curl into my palm. I want to answer, to hear his voice… but I'm also terrified. If he's cold, uncaring like he used to be, like he was this morning…

I grit my teeth, give myself a shake. I'm better than this, braver than this. He wants to be an ass? I can take it.

"Hello?" My voice is everything I could have hoped for: cool, steady, almost uninterested. Perfect Minerva.

There's a long beat of silence that makes the hair on the

back of my neck stand up. And then, "Minerva." Said in the hardest, most knowing tones.

Arne used that voice with me whenever I'd fucked up and he was going to punish me. It hardly ever happened, but I can never forget that tone.

The phone almost drops out of my nerveless fingers. "How did you get this number?" This burner should be completely untraceable.

"Are you really asking me that?"

No, I'm not. I've worked with him for five years. I know exactly what he's capable of unearthing when he wants to.

"I'm not coming back." It's the protest of a child, pathetically defiant, sad in its uselessness. But it's all I have.

Facing Callie was hard. Facing Ramona was agonizing.

Facing Arne, the puppet master behind my crimes, is unbearable.

"I wouldn't have you back." Once more, he's contemptuous. He never could stand anyone who couldn't keep up with him.

"Then why the promotion?" It's the one thing I've been puzzling over, the piece that never made sense.

"Why leave?" he asks. "We were doing great things together. It wasn't about the money for you, which I understood. I respected."

The earnestness in that makes me want to vomit. "I always meant to leave. The plan was always to betray you."

"Why? I gave you every opportunity. What went wrong?"

Everything was wrong. Every last bit of every single thing I did at Corvus was wrong. "You do evil things. You hurt people. You help others hurt people, and on a vast scale."

"You did all those things with me."

"But only to show the world what you were doing!"

"Minerva, stop being ridiculous. You're trying to ruin everything."

He doesn't understand. He can't conceive of someone

doing anything for the greater good, even if it hurts them in the process. And not only because it's not in his worldview—it's because he still sees me as Minerva.

I'm tempted for a moment to tell him what the Bastards have planned, to revel in being the one to tell him about his impending demise. That it isn't just me ruining everything—I've got others with me.

But I don't. That victory isn't mine. Instead, I'll savor what I've done to him all by myself.

"I was the mole." My voice has gone quiet. "It was me, the one you were tearing the company apart to find."

"Why would you willfully destroy something you worked so hard on?" He's getting angry now, really angry.

"If you've called to convince me not to leak everything else I have," I say, "it's too late. I've already contacted a reporter."

"Yes," he drawls, as if he knows all about it. "You should be more careful who you send things to. But the bright side is when that idiot reporter revealed it was you who sent him those documents, it provided me the perfect opportunity to get at you."

"What?" I glance out the window, see the guards still there.

"They can't stop what's coming," Arne says as if he can see me.

I don't want to know what's coming. Horror is already creeping over my skin. "What's coming?" I ask, against my will.

"Oh, you'll understand in about fifteen minutes. The point is, everything you stole is going right back into cold storage." He goes into lecture mode, his anger gone, replaced by cool triumph. "No one will ever see it unless I want them to. Our collaboration with the intelligence agencies will continue. All over the world. And you are going to prison. You're not coming out again."

The reporter burned me. They're coming for me. It's like a spike through my brain, hard, devastating. Because the story Arne has spun out is my greatest fear. And he's making it happen.

But we're not done yet. I've got him by the tail, but he hasn't landed a final bite. "I'm not the only one who has the documents. They made a copy."

Somewhere, deep in that secure facility of theirs, is the copy Finn made. Maybe someday it will see the light of day. I can see Ramona releasing it. I suppose she's earned the right to do it.

For the first time, he doesn't have a quick answer. "Who?"

"The Bastards. Finn, specifically. He's the one who planted the virus that killed the panopticon. I helped him."

There's a long, hissing exhale from Arne. "You'll die in prison," he promises.

I can't tell if he means I'll get a sentence so long I'll have no hope of freedom or if he'll send someone to give me a convenient accident. I suppose the distinction doesn't really matter.

"Maybe," I say. "But you'll never have complete control of those documents ever again."

"Ten minutes. That's all you have left of freedom."

I hear feet pounding down the dock. Someone's running and fast. This must be the thing or person he sent to deal with me. "I think it's less than that."

"Then I'll say goodbye."

I hate him and fear him and want only to bring him down… but I also spent so many years by his side. I might have been the only person in the world he trusted. It's a weird sensation to end all that. To end the strangest relationship I've ever had.

"Goodbye," I say. "They'll win in the end."

I don't have to tell him who I mean. He'll find out soon enough.

Someone, possibly multiple someones, is climbing onto the boat. They're not slowing down. The room shakes with their movements.

I set the phone down. I won't be needing it anymore.

The door opens. There's no knock, no announcement of who's there. But I suppose they don't want to warn me. I'm dangerous, after all.

I lift my chin, put on my Minerva face, and await my fate.

CHAPTER 29

Elliot bursts through the door, his hair looking like the wind tore at it.

My heart jumps into my throat.

"They aren't here yet." He's breathing so fast I can barely make out the words. "I made it."

He came for me. He's rescuing me again. Thank God he's here. I won't have to—

Oh shit. "You have to go." I shoo him away from me. I don't want him caught in the middle of whatever's about to happen. If he gets hurt or even killed… "Wait. You know they're coming?"

"*You* know they're coming?"

"Arne called—"

He grabs my hand. "There's no time. We'll talk later."

I have no idea what's happening, and there's not even a moment to think. Elliot hands me the drive, then hustles me out the door. There's a quick nod to the security guard—"Tell them whatever they want; don't get arrested for us"—and we're hurrying along the dock, away from home.

He hands me into his black Tesla, which is parked up on the curb, then shuts the door. And then we're racing off to the 280, pushing south as fast as the car can go.

Elliot drives like… like James Bond. There's no other way to describe it. Spies and bruisers and death are coming up on our tail, but he's completely in control. If I weren't on the run from the FBI, I'd find it insanely hot.

I clutch my seat, hanging on by my fingertips as he weaves around a BMW. The driver mouths something angry and obscene at us as we fly past him.

"This is very illegal," I point out to Elliot. I shouldn't have to explain to a lawyer that this is a bad idea. "I'm pretty sure some government agents are coming after me."

It makes the most sense—the reporter burned me to someone at the CIA or the NSA, they went to Arne, and he told them exactly where to find me.

"I know." Elliot doesn't look away from the road.

"You could go to prison."

"I know."

"For a long time. A serious prison, not the cushy financial-crimes one."

"I know."

Argh, nothing is getting through to him. He can't throw everything away on me. So I try the worst consequence I can think of. "You'll be disbarred."

He laughs. Longer and louder than I've ever seen. "Yes, probably."

"And you're okay with that?" I'm demanding, angry now. This is insane of him. He can't become a fugitive with me.

"No, I'm not." He cuts across three lanes, passing five cars in the process, then swings right back across all those lanes. I stop breathing for a long moment. "But I'm also not okay with your going to prison."

"The only way I'm not going to prison is if I leave the country." I've accepted that, but has he? I've had five long years to ponder my future. He still has one. At least he does if he kicks me out of the car now.

"That's why we're going to the airport. The jet is waiting."

My breath catches when I glimpse a black SUV in the side mirror. I crane around for a better look. I knew they would follow us, that they'd be right on our heels.

But the SUV fades into the distance, left behind by Elliot.

"You're still an accomplice even if you only drop me off on the tarmac." It's impossible that he doesn't understand that, but it's the only explanation for what he's doing.

He glances over at me, his gaze hot. "I'm coming with you. The whole way. We're in this together. Completely."

My throat is closing and my eyes are burning. "If you run with me, it's going to be chaos. My life from now on will be pure chaos."

He reaches over, takes my hand. Which is completely unsafe at the speed he's going, but amazingly sweet. "I'm willing to endure some chaos to be with you."

Oh God. I want to cry, to simply collapse into myself and sob. But if I do, I won't be able to hold on. And he'll get worried and he needs his entire attention on the road.

"I'm not sorry I contacted the reporter," I say. If we're going to do this, we need to clear that up.

"I know. I'm not sorry I had Finn investigate you. Or copy your drive." His voice is as clear as mine.

"I know. I did what I had to and so did you."

He opens his mouth as if to say something, but then he has to jerk the car into another lane before he smashes into the truck in front of us.

"We can't talk about it now," I say quickly. "I just wanted you to know."

"We have to trust each other from now on though." His mouth is flat, but that's because I think he's figuring out how to thread between the three cars in front of us. "We don't have to say anything more if we agree on that."

I duck my head, my heart full. We can't undo the knot, but we can work around it. Move past it. He's proved he's more than ready to do that. Hell, he's throwing away his entire life for me.

"Sure," I say. "Of course."

The words are weak, not even a match to what I'm really feeling, but it's all I can find right now.

He nods, then focuses on the road.

We arrive at the San Francisco Airport in about fifteen minutes, which must have set a new land-speed record. Elliot turns off before the main terminal, taking us to the private terminal just north of the airport. I've been through here before—but it feels strange anyway. Perhaps because I'm not pretending to be Minerva.

I have nothing, not even my passport, my heart is pounding, and my thoughts are racing. Everything feels strange and oddly new like this, cast through the prism of panic and adrenaline. But also raw and alive.

There's a man waiting at the curb when we pull up. Elliot hops out and tosses him the keys. "Take it to my brother."

The man nods.

Then Elliot helps me out. There's no security to go through, only a few people at a counter, who greet Elliot. He ignores all of them.

We race up the stairway to the jet door, taking the steps two at a time, hand in hand. Elliot's expression hasn't softened since he burst into the houseboat, but his grip on me isn't hard or fierce. More like he's there to steady me than to drag me along.

Once we're in, the steward steps out. "Just the pilot and copilot, like you requested," he says from the doorway. "The pilot will secure everything behind me."

"Thank you." Elliot leads me back into the body of the jet where a luxurious sitting area waits. There are several doors that must lead to bedrooms, bathrooms, and the crew quarters. "You don't mind serving yourself on the flight?"

I have to laugh. "I can pour my own orange juice."

He tucks me into one of the leather captain's chairs, fastening my seat belt. There's a little furrow between his eyes the entire time. "Sorry, but all this was short notice."

"How did you find out?"

He falls into the chair next to mine. He doesn't put on his own belt. "My contact at the FBI called, said that the reporter had revealed who you were and that a team was coming to arrest you. Did the reporter tell you? I'm going to have words with that fuck when we get back."

His expression shifts as if he's caught up short. Because he's realizing that it's not when we get back—it's if.

"Not the reporter," I say, distracting him. "Fuchs called me."

Elliot goes from regret to murderous rage as fast as we went down the 280. "He found the number? And had the balls to call you?"

"I didn't tell him about the takeover."

"Like I give a fuck about that." His hands are clenched on the arms of the chair. "What did he say to you?"

I actually can't even remember most of it. "He was trying to remind me of how good we were together. And then he said he told them where to find me and that everything I'd brought out from Corvus would never see the light of day."

"What did you tell him?"

I look off at nothing. That I remember very clearly. "I told him goodbye."

Elliot uncurls one of his hands from the chair arm and takes mine. "We're going to a private island where no one can follow us. You're safe from him now."

"You rescued me. Again."

One corner of his mouth quirks up. "My pleasure. Just don't make a habit out of it."

CHAPTER 30

A private island sounds amazing. Until you find yourself stuck on one, a fugitive from the law.

Emily is walking on the beach, pacing really, while I watch from a lounge chair. We've been here for three days with nothing much to do. A luxury villa, an island all to ourselves, and no one to bother us? It should be heaven.

It is, in some ways. When we come together to make love, morning, afternoon, the middle of the night. I know now I'll never get my fill of her.

But neither of us were made for leisure or laziness. There're things to do, a million buzzing events out of our reach, and it's driving us crazy.

"Have you heard anything?" she asks as she passes my chair for the sixth time in ten minutes.

"No. Nothing."

She opens her mouth on a thousand questions: *Did Fuchs thwart the takeover? Is the FBI going to show up here? What's happened to that reporter?*

But she already knows the answer to all of them, so she closes her mouth again.

"How did Finn get this?" she asks.

"The island? He bought it. Said he'd always wanted his own."

"And it's not under the legal control of any government?"

"Nope. Just maritime law."

She looks at the sky, the sand, the ocean stretching out forever. And then at the luxury villa where we're staying. "It's kind of ridiculous."

"You've met Finn. He loves ridiculous." Rumor has it he's basically rebuilt his hometown, putting in a library, parks, and even a hospital.

She comes to sit cross-legged in front of me, and I have to catch my breath. Emily in a bikini in that pose is kryptonite to my brain function.

Not knowing what she's doing to me, she props her hands on her knees. "What have you bought with all your money?"

"The boat. My car. A house for my mom."

"That's it?"

"What else would I need?"

She's confused by my answer. "You have so much money, it's not about need at this point."

"What would I spend it on?" I gesture around us. "This is not my style. But if you want one…"

She bites her lip as she smiles. "No, please don't buy me a private island. We can borrow this one. So, you're just sitting on how much money?"

I name a figure that makes her blink. And blink again.

"That's… that's a lot of whales you could save," she says finally.

True. I could also—

"Shit," I hiss as a brilliant idea comes to me. "I could buy a newspaper. And then they'd have to publish the documents."

She cocks one eyebrow. "That's beyond unethical, and you know it, Mr. Lawyer." She drums her fingers on her knee. "I guess I'm back to square one."

"We'll find another reporter. You can go slow this time

and do it out in the open." I consider suggesting contacting Callie, but if Emily wanted to do that, she would have brought it up by now. "Hell, you could even just publish it yourself. Put it all out there and let the public decide for themselves."

"No one's going to go through all those documents. And people will say they've been faked." She's not being defeatist —she's just arguing with me here. And I love it.

"They'll say that anyway. Look, we have a server here. The government can't take it down."

She kicks up some sand with her toes. "Maybe. I suppose I have all the free time to think about it now."

"You know what else you have time for?" I crook my finger at her since I can't take another moment of her looking so delectable and being so far from me.

Her mouth tilts up wickedly as she comes over and arranges herself on my lap. Instantly my cock inside my swim trunks is hard.

She wiggles her ass against my erection, which makes it worse. "Do you want sex on the beach?"

I curl my lip. "No. I don't want to be washing sand off my balls for the next week." I nuzzle her neck. "This is perfect. You in a bikini, the sunshine, the ocean. Nowhere to be."

"Does this count as one of our dates?"

"I thought we were past the date part. Now we're just… together."

She sighs, leans into my touch. "We can't stay here forever though."

"We could. I have the money saved to do nothing for the rest of my life."

"Nothing except keep your fugitive girlfriend company?"

"If that's what you want." It's not the future I ever imagined—by tomorrow I'm going to be climbing the walls thanks to all this inactivity—but then I never had the imagination to conjure up Emily. Or realize how intensely I'd feel about her after such a short time. "There are other places we could go too. I started to look into countries without extradition treaties with the US before we left—"

"Yeah, I've memorized them all." I can't see her face, but I sense her frown. "I don't want you to suffer because of me."

I gesture around us. "You call this suffering?"

She's quiet for a moment. "Don't joke. You know what I mean. This isn't you."

"It's not you either."

She cranes her neck back, looks up at the sky. "I guess we could make it us." Her fingers find mine, interlace deeply. "I'm so glad I'm not alone. I thought I could do this on my own, the same way I had all those years, but you proved me wrong."

I set my cheek next to hers. She smells of the sun and salt and sunscreen. I suppose I could handle more of this. Months, years even. If she's here with me. "I'm glad I could be here with you."

I don't regret any of it. Escaping with her was the right thing to do. Even if the law said it was wrong.

We sit like this for several moments. It's comfortable. Satisfying.

"Logan called," I say. "Still no baby."

He also had a lot to say about my running from the law with Emily, which I ignored. I told him only that we were working on what to do next and that visiting us wherever we ended up wouldn't be a hardship for him.

I also reminded him that loving a woman meant taking care of her. Being there for her. The way our father never was for our mother or for us. He shut up after that.

The rest of the Bastards haven't said anything, and Logan didn't pass anything on from them. As for the Corvus takeover, it's still ongoing. But nothing is final yet.

Fuchs remained silent on the disappearance of his

assistant. In fact, as far as the rest of the world is concerned, everything is normal at Corvus.

I did give Logan the reporter's name to pass on to Finn. Someone needs to remind that asshole that when someone gives you sensitive information, you better be real fucking careful about revealing their identity.

"They must be so excited," she says. "I can't imagine waiting for something like that, a precious thing you've wanted forever, coming any day now."

We'll do that ourselves someday. I think. It's not time yet, not with everything still hanging over our heads, but eventually.

"Anything else?" she asks quietly. Meaning *anything about our situation?*

I shake my head.

"I'm tired of doing nothing," she says with a deep sigh.

"Me too." I get up, helping her to slide down my body. I ignore my erection. "Let's go look for some more journalists."

"But the takeover..." The corners of her eyes crinkle. "I know I said I'd do whatever I wanted, but I don't want to jeopardize their plans. They're probably already pretty mad at you."

I don't know and surprisingly I don't care. "They can handle the takeover. Let's go do something for once."

Her expression is uncertain, but then she smiles. "I thought you'd never ask."

"Reporters are kind of idiots," I mutter under my breath. I scroll through the window, shaking my head.

Emily leans over my shoulder, her breasts pressing into me. The sweet thing never took off her bikini, which is lovely but also fucking with my concentration. "You can't judge them solely on their Twitter feed."

"But look at this. The moron is talking about *Marbury v. Madison,* but he doesn't have the faintest clue. That's not stopping him from running his mouth though."

Her smile is wry. "Not everyone has deep legal knowledge."

"Well, he also said here that Five Guys is superior to In-N-Out, which clearly is a sign of brain damage. I wouldn't trust him with the documents."

She reaches over and shuts the browser window. "Okay. We'll cross him off the list. Which leaves us with five other good choices."

"Let's contact them then."

"Which one?"

"All of them. Let me draft the initial contact message." I pull up a text document and start typing. Emily presses her tits harder into my back, and I can feel her nipples, firm and tight.

"Are you doing that on purpose?" I ask under my breath as I try to concentrate.

"Yes." The laughter in her voice is bright, silvery.

I turn around in the chair. "You're asking for it."

Before I can give her some teasing in kind, we both cock our heads. There's a noise outside.

Her gaze meets mine. "That sounds like a plane."

It is. "It's the jet. It's coming back."

She goes very still. Her face is a mask, but she's breathing rapidly.

"I'll see what's happening," I say. "You go into the bedroom. It's probably fine, but I'll check it out first."

She clutches my arm. "I don't want anything to happen to you."

I gently disengage. "Only the Bastards know this island exists. It's probably one of them."

And if it isn't, I'll go with whoever it is. If I can convince them to take me, that Emily isn't here, she might have a chance to flee again. It's a slim chance, but it'll be the only one we have.

At the sight of the jet coming down the landing strip, I exhale. It's our jet. Thank God.

The hatch cracks open as the crew on the island rushes up with the stairs.

Ramona appears in the doorway. And behind her is coming everyone else: Finn, Mark and January, Dev, and even Paul and Grace.

Ramona races over to hug me before the rest can join us. "Callie and Logan couldn't come."

I nod. I understand. "But why are you here?"

She leans in to whisper to me. "The guys, they all wanted to come right away. But they worried about who you're with. How she's hurt us."

"I know you don't know her like I do, but trust me, she's not what you think."

"Callie said that. She figured if you went to these lengths to rescue Minerva, that must be true. Because you don't trust."

Not even that I don't trust easily. That I don't trust at all.

"So Callie got together with me, Grace, and January, and we discussed it. We convinced the guys to come out here to help you. That we could handle it."

I lower my head. "Ramona, I—"

She pulls away. "Thank Callie. It was mostly her."

"I will. But thank you too."

She nods in acknowledgment. And then everyone's there, talking all at once. It's like being hit with a wave of glad friendship.

"Did we give you enough time?" Mark says.

"Time to what?"

"To work things out." He nods toward the villa. "With, uh…"

January nudges him. "Emily," she prompts.

"Yeah," he says.

I'm not sure what to say. They were leaving us alone to…

Finn laughs at my expression, claps my shoulder. "Don't worry, we won't stay long. But we've got a lot to tell you."

We assemble in the dining room, the only space in the villa big enough to hold us all. Emily comes out, no doubt drawn by the voices. Everyone greets her and it's only slightly awkward. But we're all trying, and that's the important thing.

Once we're all sitting down, Dev clears his throat. "Fuchs is gone," he says. "The board vote came through. Somehow, an hour or so after, he'd cleared out his office and was gone. Completely disappeared. Not at Corvus, not in any of his homes… No one's seen him since."

Next to me, Emily is rigid. Her face is pale. "He's biding

his time," Emily says. "There's no way he'll just give up Corvus."

Dev stares closely at Emily. "You had access to most of his files, didn't you?"

I don't like this, but I can't see a reason to stop him. Emily is the person who knows Corvus and Fuchs best.

"I had access to everything in the company."

Dev steeples his hands, taps his fingers together. "Would he have put a kill switch on any files?"

"Anything he considered important, yes."

"Can you disable it?"

"It depends." Emily crosses her arms. "Why?"

I lean forward, cutting into Dev's line of sight to her. "Dev, what are you looking for?"

I'm touched that they're all here, but I'm not going to let them badger Emily.

"Anything and everything I can find in his files," Dev says easily. Too easily, considering how intent he was just a second ago. "If he's going to try a comeback, we'll need the information to stop him."

Emily pulls me back, gives me a look, sweetly exasperated. "Assuming I'm not in jail, I can help."

"You don't have to," I say. She shouldn't do this because she feels obligated. Or because Dev corners her into it.

"I want to."

Paul clears his throat. "About that. I contacted a senator I know."

"A senator you bought," Mark says with a grin.

"It was a campaign donation. All legal and aboveboard since I'm a patriotic American citizen exercising his First Amendment rights." Paul quirks his eyebrows. "But a very large one, yes. Anyway, he's on the Senate Intelligence Committee. The chairman, actually. He wants to see what you have. The idea of rogue elements in the intelligence agencies fighting over something makes him want to lay down the law. Give a senatorial spanking, as it were."

That's the nastiest notion I have ever heard of. If I had ever been into spanking as a kink, it would be stone dead now.

"Really?" Emily's voice is warm with surprise. "I would have thought they'd want to bury all this."

"That was his initial impulse," Paul says dryly, "but some persuasive pressure brought him around."

I can just imagine the kind of pressure Paul put on the guy.

Emily looks to me. "Would that work?"

I consider it. "Maybe. But you don't have to do anything. You can stay here, follow the original plan of putting it all in some newspaper."

Ramona sits up. "Callie gave me a message. She says you should have come to her; she has a writer on staff who's done a ton of excellent work on Fuchs and he'd be perfect."

"I know him." Pink appears on Emily's cheeks. "I figured my going to any of you wouldn't be appreciated."

"Callie wouldn't have offered if she didn't mean it." Ramona interlaces her fingers, releases them again. "And I've been meaning to ask you about some of the programs on your hard drive. The documentation isn't great." Her voice is stiff, halting, but she makes the offer anyway.

"Sure." Emily's tone is a smidge too high. "When this is all done."

Speaking of that… it's time for me to move us forward. Into our future, whatever it may be. "I need to leave the firm. Resign as partner."

"Dude," Finn says with thick disappointment.

"You don't have to leave," Mark says. "We understand why you had to take off."

"No, it's time. This has been great and amazing… but I

never imagined doing this forever." It's the right thing, and what I want to do, but it still hurts.

Emily reaches for my arm. "You don't have to do this," she says only to me.

"I want to." I turn back to the rest of them. "I'm not going away forever," I say tartly. "Stop looking like I'm going to die."

January hides her mouth as she starts to laugh.

"You're the one who's fucking crying," Finn says gruffly.

And then we're all smiling. It's sad but happy, all at once.

Emily angles toward me, closing the distance between us. Before she can say something though, Mark is leaning forward.

"I've been considering the partner issue, actually." He glances at each of us in turn. "We need to make Anjie a partner. It's way past time."

We all very carefully do not watch Dev's reaction. Back when we first met Anjie, there might have been something between them. But nothing ever happened, even though the *thing* didn't seem to fade, at least on his end.

It's hard to ever know what's really up with Dev. Especially when it comes to Anjie.

"I'm all for it," Paul says.

"Yeah, let's do it," Finn says.

"I agree," I say, "although maybe I don't get a vote anymore."

"You'll always have a vote," Mark says. "And now she can have your office."

Finally we all turn to Dev. His face is impassive as ever. Maybe even more so.

"If that's what she wants" is all he says. His expression is a completely blank mask. Just like when he told us he'd taken over Corvus. Or when he was pressing Emily for information on Corvus's files.

"It's decided then," Mark says. "We just have to tell Logan about all this and get his vote."

Finn rolls his head on his shoulders. "After the baby comes though. And we have to get started on pulling Corvus apart."

"Apart?" Emily cocks her head.

"We're shutting Corvus down," Dev says. "Canceling all the contracts, selling off whatever divisions we can. And shuttering those that shouldn't see the light of day."

Emily merely stares at him. It's a lot to take in, because it's over. Fuchs and Corvus are finally finished.

"But… the government contracts…," she says. "The police stuff, the overseas programs…"

"It will take a lot of untangling and probably several years," Dev says, "but it will happen."

Her breathing is shaky. I take her hand, try to soothe her. "It was all for nothing," she says. "Everything I did… it won't matter. You're killing it all on your own."

I search for something to say, but nothing's coming. I feel incredibly fucking useless.

"No." That's from Grace, sharp and direct. I realize she hasn't said anything this entire time. "Everything you did mattered."

Emily looks up, her gaze hollow.

"I knew you were the mole before this," Grace says. "Fuchs wanted me to give up your identity, said he'd stop blocking my visa approval. But I didn't. Because you were doing important work inside Corvus. Work that none of these guys could do."

"My brother's case would still be hopeless without you," Ramona says softly.

"And Elliot would still be an uptight asshole," Finn says.

I bristle because I'm not *that* much of an asshole, but Emily starts to laugh. Softly at first, then more loudly. And then she collapses on my shoulder in a fit of giggles, covering her face with her hand.

I put my arm around her shoulder, hold her close. Maybe I don't have to say anything right now. Maybe I just have to be here to hold her.

Finn meets my eyes over Emily's head. "Welp, we'd better get out of here," he says. "We'll call you guys later."

I raise my hand in thanks. Emily's laughs have slowed down and now sound suspiciously like sobs.

Grace and Ramona both come over and put a hand on Emily's shoulder. She doesn't look up.

"It did matter," Grace says softly.

"Yeah," Ramona says.

I look at them with a silent thank-you.

And then they're all gone, leaving me with Emily. And a lot of decisions to make.

CHAPTER 32

I don't lift my head until after I hear the plane taking off.

I stopped crying right after they left, but I couldn't find the energy to raise my head until I knew for certain we're truly alone. I'm too raw.

Elliot has pulled me onto his lap, holding me without demanding anything. When I meet his gaze, there's a question in his eyes.

"I'm okay," I say, and I really am. "It was just a little intense. And embarrassing."

He strokes my back. "You don't have anything to be embarrassed about."

I fill my lungs with one jerking breath, then another. Until I've cleared away some of the fog of emotion. "I'm glad they came out here for you."

His hand keeps stroking. "I think they partly came for you too."

Maybe. My shoulder still thrums where Grace and Ramona patted me. They didn't have to do that, and I'm not sure if they did it for me or for Elliot.

"I don't know what to do now," I say. We had so much forward momentum, researching the reporters, preparing a contact message, even running away from the law, and Dev's put a brick wall up in front of us. "It's over now. Dev's done it all."

Elliot shifts, and I glance up at him. His expression is strained. "It wasn't just Dev," he says, "although he set it into motion. And you don't have to let him dictate what you do. Corvus may be ending, but the effects of what they did still echo through people's lives."

Meaning people will still want to see what I have, the bloody innards of a dead monster.

"Do you know this politician Paul was talking about?" I ask.

"Yes. He's…" Elliot shrugs. "He's a politician. He'll want credit for the show he'll put on with the hearings and the profiles and Sunday-morning shows and newscast spots that will come with it. But it would be the most attention-grabbing way to tell the world."

Yes, it would. There would be cameras, reporters, live streams… I might even become a meme.

"And I don't know what a federal prosecutor could offer in terms of immunity." Elliot's voice is tight. "The case the government has against you isn't going away that easily."

I lift my hand, preparing to tick off my choices. "So I can stay here, safe from prosecution, and release the documents to a reporter. It goes viral for a while, maybe Congress even holds hearings. But the people know what was going on behind their backs." I hold up another finger. "Or I go back. I'm arrested, probably, but I testify before Congress. The committee is so moved they resolve to reform the agencies, stopping the factions that wanted Corvus's programs. And I go to jail maybe."

Elliot looks like he wants to say something, but I tick off another finger.

"Or I do nothing. Corvus is done, so technically my job is done. I can fade into obscurity, try to live a normal life somewhere."

Elliot takes my shoulders, turns me to face him. "You aren't going to do any of this alone." His expression is so intent it's singeing me. "I love you."

Deep in my heart, I somehow knew—maybe when he fled the country with me—but hearing it out loud is stunning. Mind clearing, pulse stopping. A full-body reaction.

"I didn't want to presume," I say weakly. I've been alone so long my caution wouldn't let me believe. Not fully.

"It's not presumption when you're in love," he says. "It's just what you do."

Emotion is overflowing in me, surging through my chest, bubbling out of my mouth. "I love you," I say. "Love you, love you—"

It transforms into a chant before he stops it with a kiss. A kiss to blow the loneliness away on a hurricane breath, a kiss to seal us together in this always. No matter what comes.

When he lifts his head, he's staring at me with happy relief. I suppose I'm looking back at him the same way. But it feels amazing to find your other half, especially in the circumstances we did. We're allowed to look a little silly when it's just the two of us.

"I guess we should decide what to do," I say.

He catches the subtle emphasis on *we*, his eyes gleaming. "Yep. Should we take a vote?"

The easiest thing to do would be to turn our backs on all of it. To leave Corvus to crash and the rest of the Bastards to sort through the wreckage. Maybe we've done our part, done more than enough. We can go find that future together in the mountains, with our one kid.

"We could." I raise my gaze to his. "But... but we know what we have to do."

His holds me so tightly I can barely breathe.

"Go back." The conviction in his voice is exactly what I need to hear.

"Keep struggling." My voice gains strength. "Keep fighting. And if I end up in prison—"

He shakes his head sharply. "Don't say anything about
conjugal visits."

"So you won't visit me?"

"Hell, I'll be breaking into the damn prison, trying to
share your cell."

"Again, I have to point out the illegality."

His smile is crooked. "Let's talk with this senator. Open
negotiations."

I nod. "Should we go through Paul?"

Elliot frowns, a *don't doubt my prowess, woman* frown. "I
can handle a senator."

I cock an eyebrow because I can't help but needle him. He
likes it though. "Are you sure?"

"I can handle you, can't I?"

I laugh, the bright sound echoing off the walls. "Oh we
have yet to see about that. We very much have yet to see
about that."

He brushes a kiss over my temple. "I'm very much
looking forward to trying."

So am I.

CHAPTER 33

Two years later

The side room they've given us is a joke. It's closer to a closet, and the more I look at it, the more I think it *was* once a closet.

But we have privacy here, and after five grueling days of testimony, even five minutes in this closet together feels like heaven.

The senate commission has given Emily a thirty-minute break, so we ducked into our hiding spot, only big enough for the two of us. The way she immediately melted into my arms made me want to go shake the shit out of some senators.

"This better be the last day," I growl. "How long can they make you keep talking?"

The commission opened five days ago. Emily is the star witness, but first we had to hear from the reporter who burned her—she convinced me not to ruin his life, although the press has been dragging him hard—and then Deena testified. She and Emily talked briefly before her testimony, which I know was difficult for Emily. Deena abandoned her, when Emily had sacrificed everything. I don't think they'll ever be friends, but Emily seems to have made some peace with her.

There's been no time to really ask her about it though. Emily started testifying on day two. She's been answering the committee's questions ever since, about her plan to assume a new identity and infiltrate Corvus. At least it started there—we've taken several long, meandering side roads since then. I don't think a single one of these assholes has a plan for what they want to ask —mostly they just want to hear themselves talk.

"I'll talk as long as I need to," she says. She's tired though. Weary to her bones. "There's some of them that still don't see it."

"They never will," I say. "It's not in their interests to shut down these surveillance programs. Hell, they'd put up more cameras if they could. And pocket a fat donation from the camera companies."

She doesn't say anything, just sighs.

"You don't have to convince them," I say. "The whole world is your audience."

"That's not intimidating as all get-out."

I press a kiss to her hair. "You're doing beautifully. Magnificently. You're trending on Twitter five days straight now, on the cover of every major newspaper, someone publishes a story about you every ten minutes—you're famous."

"Infamous," she says, correcting me.

"That too."

"It just… I don't know what will happen. If they'll actually take action."

I don't know either. The head of the commission, Francis Church, seems very fired up about everything Emily has revealed, but the others have been… less than enthusiastic.

But they arranged for her to have immunity in exchange for testifying, and she had to hand over everything she'd taken from Corvus to the commission. No handing it over to the press.

Except there's been quite a few anonymous leaks of the documents. No one's quite sure if the leaks are coming from the senators' staffers or somewhere else. Emily and I have both professed to be very baffled by it, and Finn and Ramona have kept their mouths firmly shut, allowing us plausible deniability.

"You've done everything you could and more," I say. "Remember what you said to Ramona about one person against the system? Well, you're telling everyone about the system. And it's up to everyone to work against it. One person alone can't do it."

"I thought I could." She tilts her head back. "Do it all alone. And then I ran away to you."

"I'm so glad you did."

Before I can kiss her, the loudspeaker outside crackles on, warning us that we only have five more minutes.

Emily gives a long, loud groan. "Do you think we could just sneak out a back door?"

God, she shouldn't tempt me like that. "One more day, and then they'll release you and torment some other witness."

She cocks her head, thinking about the witness who's coming after her. "Do you think Arne will convince them when he testifies? Or even tell the truth?"

I haven't gotten over how she so casually refers to him by his first name. "I can't say what he'll do. I never understood him."

"Me either. Not really." She gently disengages from my arms. "Showtime," she says. "Again."

And then, like magic happening, her expression shifts, hardens, her shoulders going back, her spine going straight and true as an arrow. She looks fresh, as if she's just starting the day, and tough enough to last through another month of testimony.

Even now, I can hardly believe how amazing she is.

"You look great," I say.

She rolls her eyes, then winks at me, the only crack in her mask.

She doesn't know it yet, but I've made an appointment for us to look at houses up in Tahoe. And I've started to gather some cases that could use some pro bono attention—activists unjustly jailed, people fighting unreasonable bail demands, and such. With her moral compass and my legal knowledge, we could do some good in the world. We've got the money to back up our efforts too.

But first we need to get through the gauntlet of senators who never shut up.

I open the closet door for her. "Let's do this."

As she passes me, she reaches out, flicks one of the buttons of my waistcoat with her finger.

I shake my head as I follow her. Tormenting me every chance she gets.

And I wouldn't have it any other way.

ABOUT THE AUTHOR

Raleigh fell in love with billionaire romance as a teenager thanks to Harlequin Presents. She fell in love with San Francisco in her twenties thanks to how charming the city was. And she fell for a coding genius thanks to how charming *he* was.

Naturally, she had to put all of the things she loved into her romances.

You can find her online at www.raleighdavis.com.

www.ingramcontent.com/pod-product-compliance
Lightning Source LLC
Chambersburg PA
CBHW050255110726
47898CB00007B/2422